W9-CYG-293

DISCARD

That Month in Tuscany

That Month in Tuscany

Inglath Cooper

Fence Free Entertainment, LLC

That Month in Tuscany Copyright © 2014 by Inglath Cooper. All Rights Reserved.

Contents

Copyright Hardcover

Published by Fence Free Entertainment, LLC

Copyright © Inglath Cooper, 2019

Cooper, Inglath

That Month in Tuscany / Inglath Cooper

ISBN -9780578441498

All rights reserved. No part of this publication may be reproduced, distributed or transmitted in any form or by any means, including photocopying, recording, or other electronic or mechanical methods, without the prior written permission of the publisher, except in the case of brief quotations embodied in critical reviews and certain other noncommercial uses permitted by copyright law. For permission requests, write to the publisher at the email address below.

Fence Free Entertainment, LLC

Fence.free.entertainment.llc@gmail.com

Publisher's Note

This is a work of fiction. Names, characters, places, and incidents are a product of the author's imagination. Locales and public names are sometimes used for atmospheric purposes. Any resemblance to actual people, living or dead, or to businesses, companies, events, institutions, or locales is completely coincidental.

Books by Inglath Cooper

Swerve

The Heart That Breaks

My Italian Lover

Fences – Book Three – Smith Mountain Lake Series

Dragonfly Summer – Book Two – Smith Mountain Lake
Series

Blue Wide Sky – Book One – Smith Mountain Lake
Series

That Month in Tuscany

And Then You Loved Me

Down a Country Road

Good Guys Love Dogs

Truths and Roses

Nashville – Part Ten – Not Without You

Nashville – Book Nine – You, Me and a Palm Tree

Nashville – Book Eight – R U Serious

Nashville – Book Seven – Commit

Nashville – Book Six – Sweet Tea and Me

Nashville – Book Five – Amazed

Nashville – Book Four – Pleasure in the Rain

Nashville – Book Three – What We Feel

Nashville – Book Two – Hammer and a Song

Nashville – Book One – Ready to Reach

On Angel's Wings

A Gift of Grace

RITA® Award Winner John Riley's Girl

A Woman With Secrets

Unfinished Business

A Woman Like Annie

The Lost Daughter of Pigeon Hollow

A Year and a Day

Reviews

☆ ☆ ☆ ☆ ☆ **What a beautiful romance, with a huge roller coaster in the …**
By Amazon Customer on June 23, 2017
Format: Kindle Edition   Verified Purchase

My heart feels warm and gooey after finishing this lovely book. What a beautiful romance, with a huge roller coaster in the middle.

Inglath's books are pure romance, not erotica. If you're looking only for sex, look elsewhere. This is the magic of love.

The character's absolutely fabulous and we are smack dab in the middle of their feelings. Inglath knows how to write!

Keep up the great story telling.

☆ ☆ ☆ ☆ ☆ **So happy I stumbled upon this book and Author! I love her style!**
By sumgrvychk-pgh pa on January 24, 2018
Format: Kindle Edition   Verified Purchase

Stumbled upon this find while looking for expat reads. I was instantly hooked after :looking inside" and read it straight through. I can't wait to read more of this authors books! I love books I can read that completely take me away and make me feel as though I am right there in the story or watching first-hand. I adored this <3 Never a dull moment, it kept getting better and better. I especially enjoyed how it didn't end abruptly-like most reads. You know how you just really don't want it to end? This author keeps giving more and more to the last sentence. Not over-done, it is perfect! It feels complete and I have closure. No wondering or uneasiness...I am deliriously tired as it is 2 am, I am hoping I am leaving a fabulous review. :) highly recommend this book!!

☆ ☆ ☆ ☆ ☆ **Well Done Story with Great Values and Great Writing**
By Christina St Clair on August 20, 2018
Format: Kindle Edition   Verified Purchase

This was a delightful book. I loved the scenes in Tuscany. I enjoyed the characters and the story line. Truthfully, I had my doubts about a rock star, but Ren was a great character and seemed so real. I am reminded of other celebs who seem to have everything, and yet are deeply despairing to the point of suicide. The rock star and the housewife, Lizzie, form a special friendship where they do not succumb to their vulnerability by jumping into bed. It upholds the need of a woman to be true to herself -and not become submerged in the life of her husband. Finally, it presents good values about giving to others as a means of self-expression that is rewarding.

☆ ☆ ☆ ☆ ☆ **A very good writer.**
By Kindle Customer on August 24, 2018
Format: Kindle Edition   Verified Purchase

I enjoyed this book so much, that I didn't want to stop reading and go to sleep. Inglath Cooper knows how to pull you in, and keep you in, all the way through. The format of switching from character to character reminds me of Game of Thrones, but that similarity ends there. You get into the heads of all the main characters, some of whom you'll like, one you won't. There are so many elements of interest and it flows so well. And who wouldn't want to visit Tuscany? Just when you think it's all romance, you get a kidnapping. I enjoyed the read very much.

REVIEWS

☆ ☆ ☆ ☆ ☆ **A beautiful romance!**
By VavoL on October 8, 2018
Format: Kindle Edition | Verified Purchase

This is a story of a woman who is disappointed by her husband standing her up for an anniversary trip to Italy. Lizzy, the main character, feels unloved in her marriage and hopes this trip will reignite the love lost in her life. Instead, she goes alone and finds friendship and love in the beautiful Italian countryside of Tuscany. When tragedy strikes with her daughter, she returns home, trying again to piece together what is left of her marriage, but events change her life in a way she has to accept. She faces the future with her daughter, until her friend helps reunite her with the love she found in Tuscany... a wonderfully written story. The author keeps you flipping through the pages until the story is done. A great read!

☆ ☆ ☆ ☆ ☆ **I loved this story**
By Elizabeth Duckworth on March 1, 2018
Format: Kindle Edition | Verified Purchase

I loved this story, it was pure escapism. It shows that no matter what or how low you feel, something good real and romantic can happen to everyone, I know because something along these lines happened to me, although not quite as dramatic, it was comedic, romantic and had a happy ending these 40 years later. This was my first Inglath Cooper read and I will be reading more, especially on a snowy day when I want a day of idleness which we all need every now and then.

☆ ☆ ☆ ☆ ☆ **Surprise love story set in the Tuscan countryside**
By Gretchen K. Cacciotti on September 22, 2018
Format: Kindle Edition | Verified Purchase

Lizzy had planned an anniversary trip to Italy with her husband of 20 years hoping to add interest to what has become a mundane life. Husband Ty stands her up. She goes on her own and meets REN, a famous singer trying to reinvent himself. They travel the beautiful Tuscan countryside learning about themselves and each other. The tragic disappearance of Lizzie's daughter turns the experience upside down. Ty and Lizzie focus on finding their daughter. The relationship between Lizzie and Ren is renewed after the daughter is found.

☆ ☆ ☆ ☆ ☆ **Straight to the heart**
February 19, 2018
Format: Kindle Edition | Verified Purchase

Every book has deep meaning. Pulls you in and takes you to places that it straight to the heart. Ms Cooper never ceases to write incredible stories and this was just another great one to add to the list. Getting to see CeCe and Holden who!m personally are a couple of my very tops was a cherry on the top. Brava Ms Cooper can't wait for more.

☆ ☆ ☆ ☆ ☆ **Butterflies**
June 17, 2015
Format: Kindle Edition | Verified Purchase

Another romantic, yet thrilling novel that set my belly into a wave of butterflies and feely goods. The simplistic life has never looked more appealing and I feel blessed to be able to relate with it. Nothing better than a connection between a good book and your reality.

Map of Tuscany

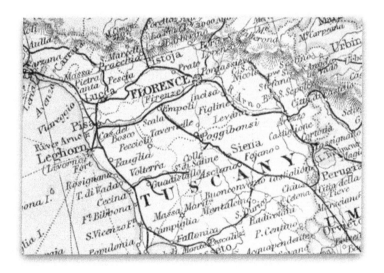

1

Lizzy

IF I'M HONEST with myself, truly honest, I will admit I knew that in the end, he wouldn't go.

But to leave it until the night before: that surprises even me.

Here I sit on my over-packed suitcase in the foyer of this too large house I've spent the past five years decorating and fussing over — picking out paint colors and rugs, which include the exact same shade, and art that can only be hung on the walls if it looks like an original, even if it isn't.

I stare at the pair of tickets in my hand, open the folder and read the schedule as I have a dozen times before.

Departure Charlotte, North Carolina 3:45 PM
Arrival Rome, Italy 7:30 AM
Departure Rome, Italy 9:40 AM

Arrival Florence, Italy 10:45 AM

My name on one: Millicent Elizabeth Harper. His on the other: Tyler Fraiser Harper.

I bought the tickets six months ago. Plenty of time to plan how to get away from the office for a month. Make whatever arrangements had to be made. Didn't people do things like that now and then? Check out of their real lives for a bit? Let others take over in their absence?

Tyler's response would be, "Yeah, people who don't care about their careers. People who don't mind risking everything they've worked for by letting some Ivy League know-it-all step into their shoes long enough to prove that they can fill them."

Our twentieth anniversary is tomorrow. I'd imagined that we would arrive at the Hotel Savoy and celebrate with a bottle of Italian champagne in a room where we could spend the next month getting to know one another again — the way we had once known one another. Traveling around the Tuscan countryside on day trips and eating lunch in small town trattorias. Exploring art museums and local artisan shops.

I shared all of this with him, and he had done a fine job of making me believe that he found it as appealing as I did. It felt as if we again had a common interest after years of a life divided into his and hers, yours and mine.

Then, a little over a week ago, he'd begun to plant the seeds of backpedaling. I had just finished putting together a salad for our dinner when my cell phone rang.

It lay buzzing on the kitchen counter, and something in my stomach, even at that moment, told me that he would back out.

I started not to answer, as if that would change the course of the demolition he was about to execute on the trip I had been dreaming of our entire married life. Actually, maybe the trip was a metaphor for what I had hoped would be the resurrection of our marriage during a month away together. The two of us, Ty and me like it used to be when we first started dating, and it didn't matter what we were doing as long as we did it together.

Ironically, we've had the house to ourselves for almost two years now. It's hard to believe that Kylie's been away at college for that long, but she has. Almost two years during which I've continued to wait for Ty's promises of less time at the office and more time at home to actually bear fruit; only they never have.

And I guess this is what it has taken to make me see that they never will.

Me, sitting on a suitcase, alone in our house, waiting for something that's not going to happen. Waiting for Ty to realize that we hardly even know each other anymore; waiting for him to remember how much he had once loved me; waiting for him to miss me.

I feel my phone vibrate in the pocket of my jacket. I know without looking that it's Ty. Calling to make sure I've canceled our tickets and gotten as much of a refund as I can, considering that it's last minute. I know that he'll also want to make sure I'm back to my cheerful self. He'll be waiting for the note of impending forgiveness in my voice, the one that tells him he doesn't need to feel guilty. I'll be here, as I always have. Things happen. Plans get changed. Buck up, and move on.

I pull the phone from my pocket, stare at his name on the screen.

I lift my thumb to tap Answer. I'm poised to do every one of the things that Ty expects of me. I really am. Then I picture myself alone in this house every day from six-thirty to eight o'clock at night. And I just can't stand the thought of it.

I actually feel physically ill. I realize in that moment that I am at a crossroad. Stay and lose myself forever to someone I had never imagined I would be. Go and maybe, maybe, start to resurrect the real me. Or find out if she is actually gone forever.

The moment hangs. My stomach drops under the weight of my decision. I hit End Call and put the phone back in my pocket. And without looking back, I pick up my suitcase and walk out the door.

~

I PARK IN THE long-term lot and not in the back, either, where Ty would insist that I leave the BMW. I park it smack dab up front, tight in between a well-dented mini-van and a Ford Taurus with peeling paint. It is the very last parking space Ty would pick and petty as it sounds, I get enormous pleasure from the fact that my door has to touch the other vehicle in order for me to squeeze out.

I get my suitcase out of the trunk, letting it drop to the pavement with a hard thunk. I roll it to the white airport shuttle waiting at the curb. An older man with a kind face gets out and takes my bag from me, lifting it up the stairs with enough effort that I wish he'd let me do it myself.

Then he smiles at me, and I realize he doesn't mind.

There are two people already on the shuttle, sitting in the back. They are absorbed in each other, the woman laughing at something the man has said. I deliberately don't look at them, keeping my gaze focused over the shoulder of the driver who is now whistling softly.

"What gate, ma'am?" he asks, looking up at me in the rearview mirror.

"United," I answer.

"You got it," he says, and goes back to his whistling.

I feel my phone vibrating in the pocket of my black coat. I try to resist the urge to look at who's calling, but my hand reaches for it automatically.

Ty. It's the third time he's called since I left the house. I put the phone back in my pocket.

When we arrive at the United gate, the whistling driver again helps me with my suitcase. I drop a tip in the cup by the door and thank him.

"You're most welcome, dear. Where you headed?"

"Italy," I say.

He lifts his eyebrows and says, "I always wanted to see that place. You going by yourself?"

"Yes," I answer. It's only then that I'm absolutely sure I am really doing this.

I am doing this.

~

THE CHECK-IN process is lengthy. When the woman behind the desk asks me about my husband's ticket, I tell her that he will be along shortly. Lying isn't something I'm in the habit of doing, but I don't think I can admit to her that he isn't coming without unraveling an explanation that might keep us both here way past the plane's departure time.

"Hopefully, he'll be here soon," she says. "Don't want to cut it too close. These international flights leave promptly."

I simply nod. She asks to see my passport, compares the picture with my face, and types a whole bunch of things into the computer. What, I cannot imagine because they already have all my information. A full five minutes tick by before she hands me the boarding pass.

Taking it from her feels like the closing of a door that I will not be able to reopen. As metaphors go, I have to think it's pretty accurate.

The security process is almost reason enough for me to stop flying altogether. If I could get to Italy by car, I would most certainly drive.

The underwire in my bra instigates a pat-down by a woman who looks as if she's no happier about the procedure than I am. She asks me in a cigarette-roughened voice if I would rather have this conducted in a private room. Since

I suppose that means she and I would be the only two occupants, I choose public embarrassment instead.

Once my bra passes the feel-up check, I am directed through the booth where I have to spread my legs and raise my arms in the same posture criminals are told to take by their arresting officer. Not for the first time, I resent the heck out of the bad people who caused all of us trying-hard-to-be-good ones to have to go through this.

An oversize purse is my only carry-on and once my laptop and camera come through the conveyor belt, I stick them back inside.

I head for the concourse that my plane will be leaving from. Boarding begins in less than an hour, so I buy a few snacks and use the ladies room. I find a seat in the chairs by the gate. It looks as if the flight will be full, based on the number of people already here. The thought of an overbooked, way-too-full flight makes my stomach drop.

I cannot remember the last time I went anywhere by myself. I'm used to Ty carrying the tickets, checking in the luggage while Kylie and I hover in the background, handing over our identification when prompted, and checking email on our phones.

I pull out my phone now and glance at the screen, noticing a text message. I click in and see that it's from Winn.

Lizzy!!! U and Ty have the time of your lives. I CANNOT wait to hear all about it. I just know u 2 are going to come back like newlyweds. Shoot,

Ty might even leave the firm, and y'all can travel around indefinitely the way u always dreamed about.

The message blurs before my eyes, the tears there before I can even think to will them away. I tap in a response.

Ty's not going.

I hit send, and it seems as if the reply is nearly instantaneous.

What?!!?

The phone vibrates. Winn's name pops up on the screen. I hit answer and put it to my ear. "Yes, I know. I was a fool to think he really would."

"Lizzy." My name is drawn out into at least six syllables. I hear her devastation. It's nearly as thick and heartbroken as my own. "What? Why?"

"A new case," I say.

"Are you kidding me?" she asks, the question lit with instant fury. While there's really nothing to be gained from it, it kind of feels nice to have someone see things from my point of view.

"I can't believe he would do this to you. It's your twentieth anniversary."

"Yes," I say. "It is."

"He doesn't deserve you, Lizzy. He never did."

"You're just saying that because you're mad. No one wanted us to be together more than you."

"Well, I was wrong. I'm a big enough person to admit that."

I almost smile at this. Ty has never had a bigger fan than Winn. In fact, I think she's been a little secretly in love with him since the day we both met him in English Lit at UVa.

"And what do you mean," she asks suddenly, "Ty's not going? Are *you* going?"

I glance around at the other passengers, and the whole thing feels surreal, like a dream I'm going to wake up from at any moment. "Yes," I say, again making my decision reality.

At least three seconds of silence tick by before she says, "Wow."

"You think I'm crazy."

"I think you're right. It's exactly what you should do. But I can't believe you're actually going to."

"There's something in there that should make me feel less than good."

"You know what I mean. How many times has he done this to you? That trip to the Caribbean after our ten-year reunion. The ski trip last winter—"

"I know," I say, stopping her. "I don't need to hear the list of times Ty has disappointed me. Because if I do, I'm also going to remember that I've pretty much been a doormat for him to wipe his feet on."

"I wish I could go with you," Winn says. "Are you staying the whole month?"

"That's my plan."

And then as if she remembers the reason I'm going alone, she says, "I'm really sorry, Lizzy. You don't deserve this. You deserve so much better."

"Spilled milk and all that," I say.

"It's his loss. One day, he's going to realize that. What did he say when you said you were going without him?"

"Um, he doesn't know yet."

Again, silence, processing, and then, "Are you sure this is Lizzy Harper?"

I actually laugh at this.

"I am incredulous. It's what you should have done a long time ago, you know," she says softly.

"Probably no denying that."

"He needs a good wake-up call."

"You know, Winn, it's not even about that. I'm doing this for me."

"Good. Good," she repeats. "How do I get in touch with you?"

"Once I leave the states, my phone will be useless. I didn't sign up for the international plan because I thought it would be nice for the two of us to cut off all communications from home for the time we were there. Ironic, isn't it?"

"But how will I know how you're doing?"

"I'll check in by email, if I have wireless."

"You promise?"

"I promise."

"I love you, Lizzy. I'm proud of you."

"You're just saying that because I'm so pathetic."

"Pathetic would be you canceling the trip."

"Yeah?"

"Yeah."

"And don't spend all of your time walking through museums and old churches and stuff. Find something fun to do. *Someone* fun to—"

"Winn!"

She laughs. "It would serve him right."

"You know that's not me."

"Maybe it should be you."

"Like that would fix my life."

"Might not fix your life, but it would definitely fix the moment."

I smile and shake my head. "You'd make a terrible shrink."

"But an excellent friend."

"I'll give you that."

"Roanoke won't be the same without you."

"It's only a month."

"Let me hear from you."

"I will," I say, adding, "Be good."

"Only if you promise not to be."

2

Ty

YOU THINK YOU know someone.

Really know them. Inside and out.

That's what being married for twenty years does. You know what your spouse is thinking nearly before she does.

Except, not this time.

This time, you have no idea what to make of this out-of-character response to not getting her way. You think of all the times in the past when things hadn't worked out as originally planned, of how she'd taken it in stride. Understood your work schedule, the competitive nature of your work and how important it was to stay ahead of the pack. To lead or be trampled.

Okay, so maybe you weren't completely honest with her about the new case load. How critical it is for you to be in the office during the next few weeks. How the timing could not have been worse.

But would she have understood? No, and so, you really had no choice but to leave it until the last minute.

Outside of your closed office door, you hear the voices of assistants and attorneys, the buzz of Finley, Harkington and Crass cases being built, others being taken apart, and you realize that you have no desire to be anywhere other than here.

This is what fills your tank.

You don't need a trip to Italy. You have no desire to see any other part of the world than the one you live in each day, thrive in each day. You love this world. And your vital role in it.

Not so for Lizzy. But then she's not a part of your world.

You're aware that you've put your own needs, your own likes and dislikes above hers, but you're the breadwinner of the family. And shouldn't that count for something?

Shouldn't your desire to stay on top of your career take precedence over touring a country you'll never see again once you leave there? A country full of old, crumbling buildings and modern cars trying to make use of archaic cobblestone streets?

You pick up the iPhone and tap redial for the tenth time in the last few minutes.

But she's not answering her phone, and you find this truly amazing. Damn it, you paid for the thing. The least she could do is answer it.

You feel the heat creep up your neck, settle at the line of your starched shirt collar, as if it has hit a sea wall.

You lean back in the chair, closing your eyes and counting to ten.

If there's anything you've never been able to tolerate, it's ingratitude. Lizzy has never appreciated the life you've built for her. For Kylie.

Always, you've felt the unspoken dissatisfaction within her. The sense that the life she lives isn't the one she'd wanted.

You'd married her, for crap's sake. You didn't have to. You could have left her high and dry to take care of a baby on her own.

Guilt instantly hits you for the thought. You love Kylie as much as Lizzy loves her. You wouldn't trade being her father for anything. But it is true that not every guy would do what you did. The right thing. The honorable thing.

And she's never given you credit for that.

You wonder now if the reason you'd finally agreed to go on the anniversary trip in the first place was because of that ever-present dissatisfaction you forever sense in Lizzy. Had you ever intended to follow through?

You don't really know the answer to that question.

Your reason for backing out, however, is a completely legit one. Is it your fault that Lizzy has never understood the word compromise?

You open the desk drawer, toss the phone inside just so you aren't tempted to call her again.

Let her get over there, see what it's like to be alone,

without a man by her side. Maybe then she'll finally see what it means to have a husband like you. A protector. A gatekeeper.

A knock sounds at the door. You straighten your tie, open your laptop and pretend to be studying the screen. "Come in."

She walks to the desk, lays a file on the stack in the corner. "I went through the brief as you asked me to," she says, her confident twenty-something gaze meeting yours and holding it.

You start to look away, but there's a flicker of something in her eyes that prevents you from doing so. "Great," you say. "I'll look over your notes later this afternoon."

"If you have any questions, don't hesitate to buzz me," she says.

Your gaze drops from her face to the neckline of her light blue sweater. The amount of skin showing is modest. This is a law firm, of course, and she's a new associate. But there's enough skin showing that you know a stab of longing to see if the rest of her is as smooth, as silky.

Neither of you say anything. You're processing this surge of attraction you feel for her. She's processing the fact that you're attracted to her, deciding, perhaps, if the feeling is mutual.

You raise your gaze to meet hers and feel the spurt of victory when you see that it is indeed mutual.

The silence clicks in and holds there. You wonder how long it would take for you to get an invitation to her apartment. Not long, you suspect. You are a partner in the firm, after all. And she's definitely interested in climbing the ladder.

Although if you had her best interests in mind, you would tell her that she should probably stick to the traditional method for getting ahead in this firm: billing every hour she possibly can.

That is the way you get noticed by the senior partners.

You should know.

But then if you had warned some of the others throughout the years, you would most certainly have missed out on some very memorable times.

She breaks the look first, as if she's felt the current of your doubt. She takes a step back, her hand fluttering at the neckline of her sweater.

And you let her go. For now.

3

Lizzy

IT'S TRULY AMAZING how much nicer first class is than coach. I've never flown it before, this trip pretty much being the splurge of a lifetime—my lifetime, anyway.

But an hour into the flight, as I'm sipping champagne and picking at a delicious assortment of olives and nuts, I decide that it is worth every penny. Every penny of Ty's, that is.

He's flown first-class across the country enough times that it's become no big deal to him. I, on the other hand, am amazed by all the space in front of me and at my sides. The seat next to me, of course, is empty because that is where Ty is supposed to be.

I'm offered red wine with my dinner, vegetarian as I had requested. I decide that it's even better than the champagne.

By the third refill, I am south of tipsy. The movie I'm watching is far funnier than I remember a review giving it credit for. I should add that I'm not a big drinker. I've always been known as something of a lightweight. Couple glasses of wine, and I'm good.

My reputation is still accurate. Three hours into the flight, I'm in the bathroom depositing my vegetarian dinner into the toilet, the nausea hitting me so suddenly that I almost don't make it to the bathroom in time.

Once I'm done, I stand in front of the slightly out of focus mirror, my hands braced on the sink, staring at my reflection. I look alarming. My face has absolutely no color, my lips nearly as pale. My forehead has that glisten of sweat left in the wake of severe nausea.

I close my eyes and will the last wave of it away, certain there's nothing left inside of me to throw up.

Once it passes, I wet a paper towel and wipe my face, fill a cup with water and rinse my mouth. Along with my dinner, I have lost every speck of giddiness loaned to me by the champagne and red wine. My head is beginning to throb like a bass beat. If I can make it back to my seat, I think I'll be fine.

I just have no idea how I'm going to get there.

I take a few moments to gather my courage, then slide the door lock to the vacant position and pull it inward. I start down the aisle and immediately feel as if I'm walking on the deck of a listing ship. Only I'm not sure if it's the floor or me that's listing.

I stumble, reaching to catch myself on a seat back when an arm suddenly shoots out to stop me.

I don't fall exactly. It's more like a collapse onto the lap of the person attached to the arm.

I squeeze my eyes shut, giving myself one second to pray this didn't really happen but was merely part of my drunken imagination. As soon as I force my eyes open, I see that it's not.

Staring back at me: a pair of blue, very blue eyes. To further my humiliation, they appear to be amused.

"I am so sorry," I say, willing myself to get up as I say the words, but finding that my legs feel like spaghetti noodles beneath me, and the plane is doing that listing thing again.

"I'm glad the stewardess had already taken away my mostly uneaten chicken tetrazzini," he says. "Otherwise, you would be wearing it on your—"

He doesn't say backside, but then he doesn't need to.

"I kind of lost my balance," I say.

His eyes light up another notch. "I noticed you were having a little trouble with that on the way to the bathroom."

My mortification is now at level ten, and the flame of it sets my cheeks on fire. I think if I put my hand to them, they will actually burn me. "I don't usually . . . I'm not a big—"

"Drinker?" he finishes for me.

"No."

"It didn't seem like you had enough to justify a bolt to the bathroom."

My vision has begun to lose its blurred edges. His face comes into complete focus. It's a rather amazing face. Thirtyish. Lean in the way of someone who's very physical.

Running? Cycling? I start to ask him which one under the lingering confidence of inebriation. I curb the impulse and clamp my teeth over my tongue, struggling once again to get up.

My legs have regained some of their musculature, but at that very moment, the plane jolts hard. A scream pops out of my throat. Before I can stop myself, I am toppling onto his lap once again.

"Ah, that was a big one," he says, sounding level-headed when all of a sudden, I'm worried.

The captain comes on then and says, "Everyone take your seats, please. Flight attendants, take your seats as well. The seat belt light will remain on until further notice."

The first-class attendant comes striding by, tossing us both a look of slight disbelief and then, "If you could please take your seat, ma'am."

"Yes, of course, I'm going," I add and then manage to get to my feet, forcing myself not to look at the man whose lap I've hijacked. "I'm sorry," I say. "Really sorry."

"Sure you're okay?" he asks.

I nod, try for a smile that doesn't happen and then slink back to my own seat, popping the belt buckle into place. I grab the blanket that I left on the seat beside me, put it over my head and lean against the window, my stomach rising and falling with every leap and dip of the plane.

I tell myself that could NOT have happened. I don't do things like this. I can't even remember the last time I had too much to drink. It's probably been fifteen years or more.

With that thought comes another.

How long has it been since I sat on the lap of an attractive man who wasn't my husband? Of course, I don't remember the last time I sat on Ty's lap either. But I know I'm not supposed to be feeling this almost painful physical awareness in the pit of my stomach.

My victim's seat is across the aisle from mine. There is absolutely no way I can take this blanket off my head until the plane lands in Rome. I lift an edge close to the window so that I can breathe and then pray that I fall asleep. Or even pass out. At this point, that would be okay, too.

~

I COME AWAKE to the flight attendant announcing our arrival in Rome.

Somehow, I've managed to sleep through the remainder of the flight and the actual landing.

I remove the blanket from my head, squinting against the onslaught of light. My mouth has that haven't-brushed-your-teeth-in-forever feeling, and I long for a toothbrush.

A bell dings, and the sound of seatbelts being unbuckled in unison prompts me to undo my own and stand on somewhat shaky legs. Memory hits me in full assault just as my gaze lands on the guy across the aisle.

He's watching me with those reluctantly amused blue eyes I now remember from the vantage point of his lap. His smile is slightly crooked and his voice low when he says, "How're you doing?"

"Ah, fine," I say in utter denial of the headache pounding against my temples like a Conga drum.

"Good," he answers.

"I . . . about the . . . I'm really sorry," I say, hoping I won't be required to finish the sentence.

"Hey," he says. "It was no big deal."

During this exchange, part of me is nodding and looking appreciative while the other part of me is processing details about him that I wish I could deny being intrigued by.

His hair, which I remember noticing last night, even through my drunken fog, is thick and longish. It's dark, the contrast to his eyes a distinct one.

Winn might tag him Beautiful Male Watching. As an art history major, she developed a habit of categorizing the guys we met in college by painting possibilities. She usually nailed them, too. Arrogant Guy Lying. Suspicious Guy Stalking. And in Ty's case, Gorgeous While Knowing It.

Beautiful Male Watching breaks the moment by standing, and it is only then that I realize how tall he is. Six-three, anyway, judging the distance he must duck in order to keep from banging his head on the storage bin above his seat.

He opens it, reaches up to pull out a backpack and says over his shoulder, "Is Rome your final stop?"

"No," I say. "I'm headed to Florence."

"Have you been before?"

"No," I say, reaching beneath the seat to pull out my bag. "Have you?"

"Yeah. It's pretty amazing."

"I can imagine. Have imagined," I say and then mentally wince at the lameness of my response.

"How long are you planning to be there?" he asks.

I'm struck mute by the question because I suddenly realize that I have no idea. The original plan was for a month, but now that I'm on the other side of the Atlantic, thinking without the confidence-building qualities of champagne, it seems ridiculous that I am here at all.

"I'm not really sure yet," I say. He's fully facing me now and having moved out into the aisle, standing straight, he's as tall as I had originally guessed.

There is something about him that seems vaguely familiar in the way of someone I might have seen before. Although I think I would have remembered him, married or not. I decide my dehydrated brain is not an accurate barometer of memory or much of anything else at the moment.

"Where are you staying?" he asks.

I feel the tilt of interest in the question. Or maybe it's only politeness. The part of me that hasn't known that feeling in a very long time threatens to send out banners of gratitude and reciprocal interest. There is weight in the moment, heavy like a pendulum that might or might not give in to the swing.

I decide that his question is merely polite conversation and the fact that I would consider the possibility that it is anything other than that is a fairly good indicator of my own parched ego. "The Hotel Savoy," I say, quickly and on the low side so that he leans in a bit as if to make sure he heard me correctly.

"Very nice," he says. "You'll enjoy it."

The departure shuffle has begun, the people behind us moving forward in small but determined steps. The plane door has been opened, and the rows of passengers at the front begin to file out.

I smooth my hand across my hair, aware suddenly that I must look an utter mess. We catch gazes again, the moment hanging there like a possibility that I know cannot exist.

It's my turn to file out. I try for a smile and say, "Well, enjoy your trip. And thanks for your . . . patience."

His smile is warmth-inducing. I think I actually feel its effect in my nerve endings. "Not a problem," he says. "You take care, okay?"

"I will," I say, and then leave the plane without looking back, putting my focus on the walkway that leads to the customs terminal. I can't deny a feeling of letdown, as if I'm driving by a scenic overlook to a beautiful place but have passed the turnoff and have no choice but to keep going.

I spot the sign that says "Baggage Claim"—Italian above, English below. I head in that direction and notice my reflection in a window.

My suspicions of horror are confirmed. My hair looks as if I slept with a blanket over my head. My face is completely devoid of any makeup. My clothes look like I've been wearing them for a week.

I repair the damage as best I can and walk to the luggage area. It takes several minutes for me to get there and when I do, I realize that most of the other passengers on the plane have beaten me to it.

It takes forever to get through customs, and when I finally step through and start looking for a taxi-stand, I hear a young girl's shriek. A chorus of yelps follows hers, and I see what looks like a group of college-age girls circling something or someone, shouldering into one another. It becomes clear then that they are getting things signed, shoulders, T-shirts, hats. One by one, they melt away from the circle, jumping up and down with ear-piercing squeals of delight.

Curious, I watch for a couple of minutes longer until the crowd has thinned enough for me to glimpse what it is that sent them into this frenzy. That's when I see Beautiful Male Watching. Pen in hand. Signing as quickly and efficiently as he can while being bumped and shouldered into by dozens of young females.

He looks up then, finds me staring and shrugs as if he's the one who's embarrassed. And then, in that moment, I realize the reason he had looked familiar to me.

He is Ren Sawyer.

Lead singer for Temporal.

My drunken topple had landed me on the lap of a rock star.

4

Ren

THE BACK OF A LIMO is one of the loneliest places a person can be alone.

I've never said as much to anyone, because I know how it sounds. First-world problems and such.

With the window up between me and the driver, I'm in a bubble. I can see the world outside, but people can't see me. I'm not a part of that world. Which is as close a metaphor to my current life as I can probably get.

I've long given up trying to convince Stuart that I would much rather grab a taxi than climb into a limousine when the whole reason I take these trips by myself is to get away from the attention. What draws attention more than a limousine driver holding up a card with my name on it?

All I want right now is a dark room and a bed where I can sleep for as long as my body will let me.

I never sleep on flights because the truth is I hate flying.

For control freaks, flying is an adventure in letting go—accepting fate and the fact that your future is in someone else's hands. I've never been very good at either.

My phone rings. I pull it from my shirt pocket, glance at the screen, and drop my head back against the seat. Gretchen. No doubt calling to make sure I haven't changed my mind about spending some time here alone. I know all I have to do is give the slightest encouragement, and she'll be over on the next plane. The fact that I do not want her to come says more about me than it does about her.

She's nice—or as nice as an over-indulged rich girl turned supermodel can possibly be. Of all people, I guess I should know what constant adoration can do to supersize a person's ego. It doesn't even seem fair to blame her.

Guilt requires me to answer the call. "Hey," I say.

"Hey," she says back. "You're there?"

"Yes. On the way to the hotel."

"Did Stuart ignore you and get the limo anyway?"

"Stuart ignored me."

"He wouldn't consider himself a good manager if he didn't. His heart is in the right place. He thinks you're safer that way. And I have to agree with him."

I start to murmur some sound of agreement, but I stop myself because I really don't want to. What I want is to disappear for a while. To not be recognized by anyone. Walk through an airport. Pick up my luggage. And disappear.

If I could do that, really do that, I'm not sure I would

come back. Smart guy that he is, Stuart knows this. It's not something we've ever talked about. But he knows it. That's why he keeps up the walls, the limousines, the five-star hotels, and leaking information on my whereabouts to reporters. He considers all of this part of his job, part of maintaining what is. And from his point of view, I get it. The illusion is held together with invisible threads. Pull one and the whole thing collapses from within.

"Are you okay?" Gretchen asks.

I hear the concern in her voice. I know if I ask her, she will say she loves me. Only I'm not sure exactly who it is she loves. The guy she thinks I am: the one who takes her to A-list parties, the one who sings in front of thousands of people. Songs he's begun to get a little tired of. I wonder if she could be in love with the me she's never had a chance to meet.

I think I know the answer. And that's what makes what we have feel thin and insubstantial.

Even as I find myself thinking this, I have to admit none of that is her fault. She can only know the guy I've shown her. The one who fits the image that's been created for me. The one I've worked so hard to make fit. Because, after all, I'm the one who went after this dream. No one made me. I think of that old adage about the dog who chased the car every day until he finally caught it. And then there was nothing to chase anymore.

If I had to name the place, I'd say that's where I am.

"I want to come, Ren," Gretchen says, breaking the silence between us. "Why won't you let me?"

"I just need a little time away. That's all."

"But you won't say how long."

"I really don't know how long," I say. Because I really don't. Long enough for this feeling of despair to dissipate. Did I really just think despair? How pathetic is that? A guy who has everything he ever wanted—and more. Despair?

But that's the word that seems to cover it. A panicky feeling of sorts that makes me wonder if I'm losing it altogether.

I think about the concert in Charlotte two nights ago. The dread that swept through me right before I went on stage. And the sensation of choking that never left me for a single minute throughout the show.

I don't know. The feeling might have started a year or so ago. Maybe a little longer. Growing incrementally with every performance until it became too large for me to ignore.

I haven't told anyone. But after what happened during this last show, I realize that fairly soon I'm not going to have to.

This time, the panic attack didn't blow up until I left the stage. Without an encore, for the first time since Temporal hit the big league.

I managed to convince Stuart and everyone else that it was a bug of some sort. That I'd gotten sick in the bathroom and already felt better.

None of that had been the truth. I suspect if Stuart didn't already know it, he did when I told him yesterday morning that I was going away for a while.

He had objected. Strongly. "Ren, we've got tons of post-tour publicity scheduled. Can't you wait a couple of weeks?"

"No," I say, my voice firm in a way that I'm not sure I've ever used with him.

He'd picked up on it immediately, saying, "All right. Okay. Whatever you need to do. It's been a long tour. You're probably exhausted."

I didn't answer that, letting my silence indicate agreement. He didn't question me again. Instead, he booked the flight, made the hotel reservation in Rome and told me to call him in a few days.

I'm not sure how long silence has again taken over our conversation, when Gretchen breaks it with, "Ren? Are you there?"

"Yes," I say. "Look, I'll call you in a day or two."

"I'll cancel my shoot in Barbados if you'll change your mind," she offers.

"You go," I say. "We'll talk when you get back. All right?"

"Okay, then," she says, her reluctance clear. "Be safe."

"You too," I say and end the call.

The limo windows are tinted, but I can still see the streets. We're passing the Coliseum ruins, a sight that never fails to unnerve me, makes me think about the fact that this is where people once came for their entertainment, most of it too horrible to contemplate.

If I have begun to think that Temporal's performances feel a bit insipid, at least there's comfort in knowing that the entertainment we provide doesn't include watching people be torn to shreds by a starved wild animal.

The limo pulls up in front of the hotel some twenty minutes later. I've stayed here several times before and know the drill. The driver tries to help me with my suitcase. I insist on taking it, handing him a fifty and thanking him for the ride.

A man in a dark suit walks out to greet me and then leads me to a private elevator and up to my room. This, too, Stuart has arranged, and I have to admit I'm grateful for this part. If only because it assures me I won't be stopped.

The man is discreet, opening my door and then handing me the key with a polite Italian-accented wish for a good stay.

"Thank you," I say, step into the room and close the door behind me. With the click of the lock, something inside me screams a quiet relief. I am alone. Finally. No pretenses to maintain. No pretending to be anything other than what I am. A guy who has created a life for himself that he no longer deserves.

5

Lizzy

I HAVE A three-hour layover in Rome. I find a café and ply myself with two espressos in an effort to stay awake.

I guess drunken sleep isn't the same as sober sleep, because I feel as if I didn't sleep at all.

The mega dose of caffeine helps, but it doesn't erase the yucky fatigued feeling.

I find myself wondering if Ren Sawyer slept on the plane. He's probably used to staying up most of the night with after-concert parties. An overnight flight would be lightweight to him.

Every time his name pops into my head, my cheeks instantly ignite with embarrassment. It was bad enough to think that I had subjected myself to the mortification of a drunken topple onto a stranger. That was enough to last me several lifetimes, but add to that the now undeniable fact that the stranger had been the superstar my own daughter had lusted after throughout her high school years, well, that put it into the realm of what did I do to deserve that?

Not that it would likely ever cross his mind again.

But it would certainly cross mine.

I force my attention to the book I've been trying to read on my iPad. Every other line or so, the words start to blur, and my intention of putting my mind on something else fails.

Instead, I open my laptop, turn on the wireless and find a hotspot to log on through. Since my phone doesn't have service, I fully expect a blistering email from Ty. And there they are, three of them, the subject line in capital letters: CALL ME NOW!

I open the messages to find nothing other than the subject, and something about the demand has me exiting out of my account and slapping the laptop closed.

At least I no longer need to wonder if he's angry.

Which, if I let myself think about it, will send me right over the edge.

Ty's decision not to follow through on this trip he had promised we would take together was his own choice. The fact that he had assumed I would do what I've always done, fall in line with his choices, well that was his to live with.

As for me? If I needed any further impetus to stay here for the next month, to not let guilt weaken my resolve and walk me over to the ticket counter for a reroute home, he has just given it to me.

I am here. I am staying. If it kills me, I will enjoy myself.

6

Ty

YOU HOPE SHE'S already starting to regret her rashness.

She's barely ever traveled anywhere without you or Kylie. The Lizzy you know was never a chance taker. She'd always been the one to read aloud articles about Americans who had horrible disaster vacations while outside the country.

There had been that cruise ship that hit a rock off the coast of Italy and capsized. She'd even made you and Kylie watch a documentary about the whole thing. And she'd vowed never again to get on a cruise ship.

You finally give up on sleep at five-thirty, get up and take a shower, then head to the kitchen to make coffee. Normally, Lizzy has it ready for you. After numerous edits over the years, she now makes it exactly as you like it—from coffee beans. Very hot. Very strong.

You don't add enough coffee, and the first cup is far weaker than you like. You ditch the whole pot and start over.

You find yourself resenting her for putting you in this position. She should be here, making coffee the way she always does. It's not your job, anyway. Your job is to get up and go to work, not in a state of frustration, but ready to meet the challenges of what are often very challenging days.

You feel the heat of anger light your cheeks again, and suddenly, you really want to hit something. Instead, you walk outside, get the newspaper and bring it back to the kitchen table where you sit with your mildly improved coffee.

Just as you open the first section, your cell phone rings from its spot on the counter. You get up quickly, sure it will be her, asking you to get her on the next flight home. She made a mistake. She should have known better.

But a glance at the screen shows Kylie's name and picture. You consider not answering. Explaining all of this to her right now seems like more than you can manage. But if you don't answer, she'll just call back.

You swipe the screen and put on a bright voice. "Hey, sweetheart. You're up early. How's everything in Charlottesville?"

"Good. Are y'all in Rome?" she asks, yawning.

"Ah, no," you say, "at least I'm not."

She's silent for a moment as if she's not sure what to make of your answer. "You're not?"

"I wasn't able to go on the trip. A case needed my attention at the last minute."

"Oh. I know Mom must have been disappointed not to go."

"Yeah," you say. "About that. She went alone."

"Mom?" she says, expressing the same incredulity you felt on learning of it. "No way."

"Way, I'm afraid," you say.

"I can't believe you let her do that."

"I didn't have a lot to say about it."

"You didn't know she was going?"

"No."

Silence stagnates on the line. You suddenly feel the need to break it, to lessen the implications of Lizzy making such a choice. "I'm sure she'll be fine. She's wanted to do the trip for a long time."

"I know. But that doesn't sound like Mom. Can you go over and join her at some point?"

"I'm not really sure," you say, trying to keep your voice even, unmarred by the anger still lighting a flare in your chest.

"Is she sticking with the original itinerary?"

"I would assume so," you say, and then wish you could take that back. It sounds so spineless, so wimplike.

"Dad. Is everything all right between you two?"

"Everything is fine."

Silence again, while your daughter weighs whether to believe you or not. But you know she will. Because you're her favorite. She always sides with you.

"I can't believe she wouldn't reschedule the trip so that you could go too."

There. Just as you'd thought. You have her sympathy. "It's okay, honey. I've got plenty of work to keep me busy."

"All work and no play—"

"You know they're practically the same to me."

"Yeah, I know. Well, call me if you want me to come home for the weekend."

You start to say that's a good idea, but then you picture the new associate, that smooth skin above the neckline of her sweater. Instead, you say, "I suspect I'll be in the office most of Saturday and Sunday. Otherwise, I'd take you up on it."

"Are you sure?"

"Yeah."

"Okay. I'll be checking on you."

"Thanks, honey."

Once she clicks off, you stand for a moment, staring at the phone. Shouldn't you feel a little bit of guilt for deceiving your daughter?

Yes. You wait for it to hit, but it doesn't.

You stick the phone in your pocket, grab your briefcase and head for the door.

7

Kylie

KYLIE HANGS UP from the phone call with her dad, feeling as if she never saw that one coming.

She's sitting on her bed, staring at the screen of her phone when Peyton, her roommate, opens the door and slinks into the room.

"Dare I ask where you spent the night?" Kylie asks, looking at her with a raised eyebrow.

"Probably better if you don't," Peyton says, flopping down on the twin bed beside her. "What did you do? Study all night?"

"Imagine that. This being college and all."

"Ooh. Kylie's snippy this morning. I like it."

"Shut up," she says and swats Peyton's arm. Kylie smiles despite herself. Most of the time, she's irritated at Peyton.

She's like a toddler who constantly gets into trouble, but has become expert at charming her way out of it.

"So what's the source? Your mom call?" she asks, looking at the phone in Kylie's hand.

"No," Kylie says quickly, and then, because she feels a desperate need to talk about what had just happened, adds, "My dad."

"Isn't he the one you get along with?"

Kylie shrugs. "It's not that my mom and I don't get along. She just kind of smothers me."

"Isn't that her job?"

"Maybe when I was five. I'm not five anymore."

"In her defense, loving someone and wanting the best for them can cause overprotectiveness. It's a known fact."

"And all the side effects that go with it."

"There is that."

Kylie hesitates and then says, "My parents were supposed to take this great twenty-year anniversary trip to Italy. My dad had work stuff though and couldn't go at the last minute, so my mom went without him."

Peyton leans back, raises a finger. "Score one for Mom. And you think there's something wrong with that?"

"Yeah, I do. She could have waited and gone another time."

"Hmm," Peyton says. "If he's anything like my dad, there won't be another time."

"My dad's not like that. He just takes his work seriously."

"So does mine. Which means my mom spends a LOT of time alone. I am so not going to marry a guy like that."

"Then he'll have to be independently wealthy to support your Starbucks habit."

Peyton giggles. "That'll be the least of his worries," she says, stretching out a leg to show off the Prada platform she'd worn out last night.

"You got that right," Kylie says.

"Is your mom in Italy now?"

"I guess so."

"Why don't you call her if you're all worried?"

"I'm not worried. More like pissed."

"Por quoi?"

"Because she shouldn't have done that to my dad."

"My guess is that's exactly what she should have done."

"Hey. Whose side are you on anyway?"

"Well, I've seen my mom after one of my dad's last minute cancellations. She takes it pretty hard. Maybe your mom did, too."

"I don't think my parents are like yours."

"How so?"

Kylie shakes her head. "I don't know. You know how when you're a little kid, you think your parents love each other more than anything in the world? That nothing could ever change that?"

"Yeah, I do."

"Somewhere along the way, I figured out that was all just a big fairy tale."

"Hey," Peyton says, putting her hand on Kylie's arm. "I know what you need."

"What?"

"Let's ditch classes today and go shopping—with your parent's credit card. That should make you feel better."

"You're crazy," Kylie says.

"But I'm right."

Kylie doesn't bother to deny it.

8

Lizzy

WHAT I ABSOLUTELY love about Florence: the bells.

The magnificent sound of church bells waking me in the morning. A heavy medieval *gong, gong, gong* that is as pleasant as it is beautiful, music I would like to hear over and over again.

As soon as the bells rouse me from sleep, I jump out of bed and open the glass-pane doors so that I can hear them in their fullest glory. I think it would be wonderful to be woken this way every day of my life.

The second thing I love about Florence: this room. This magnificent, high-ceiling room in the Hotel Savoy. Again, another piece of our anniversary splurge. The room is far more luxurious than anything I need. Nonetheless, I love it. I love, too, the fact that the doorbell rings at seven on the dot, and a dark-haired Italian, who looks like he must be a college student arrives with my tray of American coffee. It's a weakened version of their Italian espresso, but still strong for me. The taste is wonderful, rich and mellow on my tongue. A small basket of delectable pastries accompanies the coffee pot. They all but melt in my mouth.

I pour myself a cup and sit on the terrace of my room that overlooks a square, where people are walking quickly in every direction. There's a woman ducking into a bakery. I smell the goods from here, warm bread and something sweet, like doughnuts. A man with a white cane and a seeing-eye Standard Poodle expertly taps his way through the middle of the square. I'm amazed that, of all the people winding in and around him, he never stumbles, never even brushes shoulders with anyone.

All of the streets within my immediate view are pedestrian only so there's no roar of cars to disturb my interpretation of this extraordinary spring morning.

My third favorite thing about Florence: the food. It is incredible. In even the smallest, plainest trattoria, you can find the best meal you've ever eaten. Homemade pasta with a pomodoro sauce that tastes as if someone just picked the tomatoes from a summer garden, the olive oil fresh and fruity.

Last night, I had dinner at a little place I happened to pass on my way back from the Ponte Vecchio where I had browsed the wonderful jewelry shops that occupy either side of the famous old bridge.

The décor of the trattoria was simple and rustic, heavy wood tables and comfy farm-style chairs. I sat by a window where I could see the people passing by and took my time eating. The owner of the trattoria walked from table to table, welcoming people. I was one of the few Americans there, but when he approached me, he did so in English and asked me what I thought of the dessert. I told him that I wasn't sure I could find words to express it well enough, and it was clear this pleased him greatly. When I left, he asked me to come back again, and I said I most definitely would.

I am now beginning day three of my stay in Florence. There's something about the immediate absorption of the beauty in this place that makes it feel as if I've been here much longer.

I have done nothing more with my days than wander street to street, not even using a map, letting them lead me where they would. Passing shops with beautiful leather goods, journals, satchels and purses. Shoe stores in which I want no fewer than a dozen pair. And bakeries with the most mouthwatering breads I've ever seen—mounds of them fresh from the oven.

Two full days of this. In my adult life, I have never known such a luxurious expenditure of time. In fact, not since my childhood when a day knew no schedule aside from play and sleep. Certainly not in my regular life where a day is normally sectioned off by appointments and fundraising meetings and grocery shopping and all of those things that somehow manage to steal most of the best parts of our waking hours.

I wonder how it is that we go along year after year never questioning the routines we've set for ourselves, never wondering if it could be different. I feel as if I've opened a door and discovered a way of life that makes so much more sense to me. A slower pace that allows me to actually see the beauty around me. Hear the song in the sounds and feel appreciation for it all.

I take another sip of my coffee and wonder if this would have been the same for me had Ty actually come. I have barely completed the thought before admitting the answer. No. It would not have. With Ty, there's always a sense of impatience to get to the next thing. The next case. The next rung up the law firm ladder. He is constantly checking his watch, and I've wondered many times if it's because he would rather be doing something other than what he is doing with me at that moment. If I'm honest, I've wondered if there was somewhere else he would rather be. Someone else he would rather be with.

Whatever the reason, this habit of his makes everything we do together feel rushed and incapable of comparing to whatever it is that he's anxious to get on to. I realize now that to wander Florence without a schedule would make no sense whatsoever to Ty. He would see it as a place to be conquered. The most famous tourist attractions viewed and checked off a we've-done-that list. So that in the end it would seem more about completing the list than actually seeing what there is to see.

Before coming here, I really didn't question that. It is Ty's nature. It's who he is. If it wasn't who I am, somehow that failed to be significant, at least in any way that matters.

The sun is now draping itself across the terrace, its warmth caressing my face. I lean back in the chair and close my eyes, willing myself not to think about Ty. Even as I do, a thorn of worry makes itself known.

I haven't let Kylie know that I took this trip without her daddy. I have no idea if Ty has done so. My guess would be yes. Guilt prods me out of my chair. I retrieve my laptop from the room and bring it back to the terrace, popping the lid open and waiting for it to find the hotel's wireless signal.

Once it does, I log in to my email account. Surprisingly, there are no new messages from Ty. But there is one from Kylie. I open it with some reluctance. Selfishly not wanting her certain disapproval to pop my bubble of happiness. Even so, I cannot help but read what she has written.

Mom,

Daddy is worried sick about you. Please call him as soon as you get this. I can't believe you went without him.

K-

And there it is—the instant feeling of something almost like shame.

It's not the first time Kylie has put me in my place. As an only child, she's really good at manipulation.

But maybe that's more my fault and Ty's fault than it is Kylie's. At some point in her childhood, and I'm not even sure I could say when, a tug of war for her affections had come into play between Ty and me, each of us seeking her approval whether we realized it or not.

I wonder now if that was the first symptom of erosion in our relationship. The need to prove to the other who was more valuable in our family structure.

If I had to say which of us pulled ahead at some point, I will admit it was Ty.

Before age twelve, Kylie was Mama's girl. I could do no wrong in her eyes. She wanted to dress like me, smell like me.

How many conversations did we have–in the car going grocery shopping or a trip to the library—about how she would never leave home? That even after she got married, she and her husband would live with us. Maybe they could build another part to the house, she said, but she would never leave home. And she would only marry someone who would agree to that.

As the adult, I knew it was simply her age talking. That the picture she painted was nothing more than a fairy tale. But it felt so nice to be that loved by her—to think that she never wanted to be apart.

And then, not that long after she turned twelve, things started to change. They were little shifts in the beginning. Like the tremors way down deep in the earth, predicting a quake to come. I felt them like pinpricks to the skin. One night when we'd gone out to dinner, she said my dress looked frumpy. A year before, she had called that same dress classy in the way Coco Chanel thought women should dress.

Frumpy hurt. It sounds silly, and I could admit it even then. But there was a change in the tide.

At the same time, Ty grew in stature where Kylie was concerned. She wanted to know more about what he did every day. Became fascinated with the trials he was a part of, with the criminals he had represented in various cases.

And while she had once wanted to be a photographer, like I once was, now she wanted to be a lawyer, like Ty.

He would take her with him to the office on Saturday mornings, letting her read depositions, giving her some minor task to complete within them. She would come home elated by the fact that she had helped him and earned his lavish praise.

And as Ty began to be the recipient of her obvious affections, I became diminished in her eyes.

At thirteen and fourteen, it seemed that a day never passed that we did not end up in an argument over some difference of opinion about what she should or should not wear to school. Tank tops that showed cleavage. Skirts that were inches from being close to meeting the dress code. And boys. That was probably the biggest divider. Kylie wanted to date. Like all her friends were doing, she said. Being dropped off at the movies or at the mall to wander around hour after hour, hand in hand.

Ty and I had always agreed that she would not date until she was sixteen. This was the restriction my mother had set for me. And it was one I came to believe in because of how close I got to doing something extremely stupid when I was thirteen, and a seventeen-year-old boy wanted to take me out. Of course, I thought I should be allowed to go. My mother, however, stood her ground and would not relent.

I shared this with Kylie several times, but to her, there was no comparison between the world she lived in and the teenage world I had lived in. They might as well have occurred on different planets for as relevant as she found my advice.

The gap of distance between us continued to increase to a point of actual heartache on my part. If I had hopes of maturity bringing new focus to Kylie's attitude, it was completely lost on the day she turned sixteen.

She had asked to borrow one of my sweaters for a party she was going to that night. I told her where it was in my closet, and she had run upstairs to get it. I had been busy making her cake in the kitchen and didn't notice how long she'd been gone until I glanced at the clock and realized it had been almost an hour.

Concerned, I called up the stairs but did not get an answer. I walked up, looked in her room and found her in my closet.

She was sitting in the middle of the floor, holding the red leather diary I kept as a teenager. I stared at her, my lips parting without any sound coming out. I finally managed to say, "How . . . where . . . how did you find that?"

"A button popped off the sweater, and I couldn't find it, so I looked under the dresser. I saw this, stuck up under the drawer."

"That's mine. You should have asked first."

She'd closed the cover, softly, too softly, looked at me and said, "Why did you never tell me?"

"Because in the end, Kylie, it didn't matter."

"You getting pregnant and only getting married because of that doesn't matter?"

"Your daddy and I would have gotten married anyway. Surely, you know that."

"No, I don't know that. And that's not how it looks. Here," she said, opening the diary and flipping to a page where I knew exactly what I had written. "I wish I had never said yes," she read.

My heart caught in my throat. I struggled to find the words to explain to her. "Oh, Kylie, I was nineteen years old, barely a sophomore in college. I was scared of what my parents would say. Scared of having a baby. Scared of letting go of every dream I had for myself. That was who wrote those words—a very different me from who I was after I figured out the right thing to do."

"And what was that?" she'd asked, tears in her voice.

"To marry your daddy and to have you. So that is what I did."

She looked back at the page, her eyes taking in the words. "But you weren't even sure that you loved him. That's what you said here."

"I wasn't that much older than you are now. Try to understand that—"

"You try to understand, Mom. You try to understand that

what I thought was true about you and daddy wasn't true at all."

"I love your father," I said. "You know I do."

"I've always wondered, you know," she'd said, rubbing a thumb across the cover of the journal. "I knew there was something."

"Kylie, don't," I said, starting to reach for her.

"No. *You* don't," she'd said, tossing the journal at my feet and running from the closet and out of the room.

I leaned against the wall, slid down to the floor with my knees bent against my chest. I felt as if someone had taken a wrecking ball to a life I had so carefully put together. It lay around me in shards and smithereens, and I wondered if Kylie's anger would ever dissipate.

Things between us were never the same after that day. I had tried so hard to fix things with her. But she had closed a door between us, and no matter how many times I tried to explain why we hadn't told her, she was unyielding in her refusal to let me in again.

Her relationship with Ty, however, continued to flourish. She spent even more time with him at the office when she wasn't in school. In her eyes, he was everything that she wanted to be. He had her respect and admiration, and I had neither.

To say it hurt came nowhere near describing how her rejection felt. I kept telling myself that eventually things would smooth out again, and she would forgive me for whatever wrong she thought I had done.

I couldn't bring myself to ever talk to Ty about what had happened that day. To do so would mean telling him what Kylie had found and admitting the awful doubts I'd had after finding out that I was pregnant. Somehow, digging all of that up again, reexamining it with Ty possibly reacting in the same way Kylie had . . . I didn't have the courage to do it.

I stare at the computer screen now, my daughter's words at the bottom of the email.

I can't believe you went without him.

I imagine the conversations the two of them have had about what I've done, that maybe I've gone a little crazy because this is so out of character for me.

I hit Reply and begin an email laced with apology and reassurance.

Dear Kylie,

I know this must not make any sense to you. And I'm sorry for any worry I've caused. Please understand that this was something I've always wanted to do. Your daddy decided that he couldn't go, and so I'm visiting a place I've always wanted to see. I will be in touch soon.

Love,

Mom

I hit Send and hear the whoosh of the email as it flies from my inbox to hers.

A yawning feeling of loneliness settles over me. I wonder how it's possible to reach this point in life, married with a family, and be this lonely.

I hate my own self-pity. I mostly refuse to allow myself to indulge in it. But I can't deny that it hurts. I wonder, not for the first time, if it's always going to be this way. Ty and Kylie on one side of the fence and me on the other. The thought swamps me with an awful feeling of regret.

I start to close the laptop, spot my cursor blinking in its nosy Google search box. My hands automatically slide to the keyboard.

I type in his name. Hit Enter. And blink at the number of results returned by my search: 6,897,512.

That really shouldn't be a surprise, I guess. He is, after all, a rock star.

Ren Sawyer. Lead Singer. Temporaltheband.com.

Every time my encounter with him pries itself into my thoughts, I instantly light up with the heat of embarrassment. Until now, I've resisted the urge to find out anything more about him. I can't really say why I've given in to curiosity now. Rebellion, maybe? In response to Kylie's email? I don't know. Maybe that's just an excuse. Maybe it's just old-fashioned curiosity.

I click on the first link to an article in *USA Today* about the conclusion of a recent tour. There's a photo of him at the top of the page, a gorgeous young woman, I vaguely recognize as a model next to him.

In the caption below, her name is linked with his, and I realize who she is. Gretchen Macher. She certainly looks like someone who would be with him. It would be hard to say who was more beautiful. Him or her.

I almost talk myself out of reading the article, but my gaze is pulled to the type.

By most accounts, the Temporal tour came to a highly successful conclusion on its last stop in Charlotte, North Carolina. Ticket sales for the thirty-city tour topped the group's previous records. Speculation continues as to whether the group will produce another album. Band manager Stuart Langston is quoted as saying, "There is no question as to whether the band will go to the studio for another album." Questions have surfaced regarding the performance of lead singer Ren Sawyer at the tour's last concert in Charlotte.

A concert-goer, who had flown from Minneapolis to see the show with tickets for front-row seats, told a Charlotte newspaper that "something went very wrong in the last two songs." She claims that Sawyer became pale and shaky. Having attended a concert in every one of the band's individual tours, she stated, "I have never seen him leave the stage and not return for an encore."

Questions directed at the band's manager were dismissed as nothing more than unfounded speculation.

Sawyer's current girlfriend, model Gretchen Macher,

was seen in New York City last night at Club Scout with another member of the band, drummer Tommy Rainieri. Sawyer was said to not be in attendance.

I click out of the article, feeling a little like a voyeur peeping in through a window to Ren Sawyer's personal life. Granted, the article appeared in *USA Today* for anyone to read. Even so, I feel as if I've wandered into someplace I shouldn't be.

This time, I follow through with closing my laptop, getting up from the desk chair and walking back to the terrace for a last sip of now lukewarm coffee.

The street below has come to full life, tourists wandering among the locals headed for the next attraction on their checklists.

I don't want to think about him. But I can't seem to stop myself from wondering what happened at the end of the concert in Charlotte. The concert that had taken place the night before we flew across the Atlantic on the same airplane.

I try to think if I had noticed anything similar to what the concert-goer described, but my memory would not be the most accurate considering my state of inebriation.

Even so, he had seemed normal, whatever that is for a rock star. I have to wonder what exactly could be so horrible in a life like the one Ren Sawyer leads. Fans waiting for him wherever he goes. A supermodel girlfriend on his arm.

And, too, the recognition of being really great at something you love to do.

Maybe like most lives, that is simply the surface, the outer coating the rest of the world sees that in no way suggests what might be beneath. I suppose my own life is a good example of this.

On the outside, I have pretty much everything a woman my age could want. A successful husband. A beautiful, intelligent daughter. An enormous house in a great neighborhood. If you're standing back looking from a distance, it does look really good. I can't deny that.

But there are cracks.

I feel a little ashamed in admitting this because maybe I really have nothing to complain about. No one has a perfect life. Not even, I suppose, someone like Ren Sawyer.

I wonder if his girlfriend will be meeting him in Rome. If maybe she is already there. Will she be able to help fix whatever went wrong for him at his last concert?

If I had to guess, I would say yes. What man wouldn't allow himself to be fixed by someone like her? But then, I think about my own hurt. I wonder if it is even possible for someone else to fix us. If maybe, it is only possible for us to fix ourselves.

9

Ren

I SLEEP FOR thirty-four hours straight. If you don't count getting up to go to the bathroom three times and twice for a glass of water.

This time when I start to wake, I'm no longer tired. I feel that immediately. The leaden weight of physical fatigue is gone. I wait, hopeful that the mental fatigue will also be gone.

But the weight on my chest is still there, heavy, gray, and I'm suddenly angry to acknowledge its presence. I want it gone. I hate what it does to me. Hate how I do not have the energy to push it away. I know I should. I just cannot find an angle from which to attempt to get enough leverage to move it. Every possible avenue for escape seems an impossible effort.

The curtains in the room are closed, but the seam at the middle where the two are pulled together is broken by a crack of sunlight. I need to get up. I will get up. I will order coffee. Take a shower. Eject myself out of this room and into the world. A ball cap and sunglasses, and I will go mostly unrecognized.

Here, I can wander the streets alone. At first, this sounds good to me. Alone means no pressures from anything related to the business. No decisions to make. No arguments to settle between band members. This is what I've wanted. And I tell myself it will be good.

I roll over, swing my legs to the side of the bed, and sit up with my elbows on my knees. That's when I think of her. The woman I met on the plane coming over. I remember her face in the airport when she'd seen me standing in the middle of all those screaming girls. The surprise that widened her eyes, made her lips part slightly.

I had liked it better when she didn't know who I was. I'd seen the transformation in her face the way I had seen it in others too many times to count. Before, she'd thought I was some regular guy she'd had a moment with. A moment that, under other circumstances, we might have both acted on.

Once she'd seen the other me, the one signing autographs for teenage girls, all of that had melted away, as if it never existed.

I call downstairs, and the coffee arrives in minutes, even though it's one o'clock in the afternoon. I down three cups and wait for the caffeine to kick in.

I spend a good fifteen minutes in the shower. One, because it feels good to get clean again. And two, if I'm honest, because getting out will mean having to follow through on leaving the hotel room.

I finally force myself out, dry off and then wrap one of the hotel's extra thick towels around my waist. I wipe the fog from the bathroom mirror, and there I am, staring at myself.

I could use a haircut. My eyes are red despite all the sleep. I wonder what's happened to the energy I once saw in my own gaze, the energy that pulled me forward day to day, made me want to reach for the next rung with the kind of determination that didn't take no for an answer.

It's gone. I can see that. Feel that. In the mirror, I see a shell of my former self. Breakable. Weary.

I unzip my leather shaving case, pull out my toothbrush and a tube of toothpaste and brush my teeth. I reach in the case for a razor, and my hand hits the plastic bottle I haven't let myself think about since putting it in there after the concert in Charlotte.

I pick it up; stare at the label where my name is written.

PRESCRIBED TO: REN SAWYER. THIRTY TABLETS.

Only there are sixty. Two bottles in one because I deliberately held on to a month's worth before having the prescription refilled.

I stare at the bottle for a long time, thinking how easy it would be to down the lot of them and simply go back to bed. Not have to live another moment with the guilt eating a hole inside of me. The lure of this option is so tempting that I have to anchor my hands to the sink counter to keep from giving in to it.

I hear my brother's voice, the promise we'd made to each other when we first started to hit it big. "So here's the deal," Colby had said one night after we'd just written a new song together. "No alcoholism. No drug habits. No ending up dead in a hotel room. Promise me neither one of us will end up a rock-and-roll cliche."

At the time, it hadn't seemed like such a difficult thing to promise. Drugs and alcohol had never been our thing. Women? Well, that was a different story—for us both.

I let myself picture the headlines. **Temporal Lead Singer Found Dead in Rome Hotel**.

I cram the bottle back in the case, zip it shut and shove it inside the cabinet below the sink.

I get dressed quickly, jeans, t-shirt, ball cap. I grab a pair of dark sunglasses from the backpack I'd carried on the plane. I take the elevator to the lobby, walking through the main area without meeting eyes with anyone.

I start to think I'm home free, stepping outside into the sunlight only to spot a group of teenagers hanging out at the foot of the steps. I hope like hell they're not there for me.

I aim for the other side of the stairs, ducking my head and walking fast. Just then I hear a gasp, followed by a squeal and then suddenly the entire circle of girls is running at me. I curse Stuart for leaking my stay here. And also for what he would expect me to do, now that I've been found.

Stop. Smile. Sign. Be thankful for fans.

That is exactly what I've done for the past ten years. As if there's actually a manual for this kind of thing, and I am its poster boy.

I nearly stop and turn around. Almost. But then something explodes inside me, and I'm suddenly running, full out, down the sidewalk, until I hang a right onto a narrow, cobblestone street. It's one way, and cars are coming toward me. I hug the side of the building to my right and keep going, ignoring the horns honking around me.

I glance over my shoulder. Three of the most determined girls are following me. They're doing a fine job of keeping up.

"Wait!" one of them calls out in an English accent. "Ren! We just want your autograph. We've bought all your songs!"

I continue to run as if I've been doused in gasoline, and they're carrying flaming torches.

I'm only too aware of how easy it would be to hate me for this. How many guys wouldn't welcome the opportunity to be chased down an Italian street by three girls? Had it really been that long ago when I loved the attention, the adoration? When it somehow, even if temporarily, filled the hole inside me that seemed to not quite believe that any of it was real?

I don't slow down until I no longer hear the click of their heels on the cobblestone street. I glance over my shoulder to see that they are no longer anywhere in sight. I begin to walk, dragging in ragged breaths that tell me how wrong I was to slack off on my running.

I want to lean against the closest wall and slide to the

ground, but I force myself to walk, one foot in front of the other, step after step until my breathing begins to slow, and my chest no longer aches. I've reached a square by now that isn't one I recognize. Several people are throwing Frisbees to their dogs. Other people sit on benches, watching, eating bread, sipping from bottles of water.

I seek out the closest bench, sit down and glance around the perimeter of the square to make sure the girls haven't caught up with me. I feel my phone vibrate in my back pocket. There's a text from Stuart.

WTF, Ren? They've been waiting two days for you to come out.

I consider not answering at all. I don't have to. But fury prompts my fingers to the keys.

Did you not understand what I meant when I said I wanted some time alone?

You're mostly going to get it. A few public sightings to keep you on your fans' radar. What's the harm in that?

I want to be off radar. That's why I'm here.

Nobody understands what's going on with you, man.

Nobody needs to. I trusted you, Stuart.

I'm sorry, Ren. It won't happen again.

No. It won't.

I send the text and turn off the phone altogether. I stick it in my pocket and head back to the hotel. I stop in a little shop along the way, buy a new hat, a jacket and some different glasses.

Just before reaching the hotel, I stop at the corner where I have a clear view of the entrance. The girls are no longer there. I suspect it's because Stuart has gotten worried enough to call his spies at the hotel and warn them to make everyone leave.

I can't say that I'm sorry, but it's too little, too late.

I take the elevator to my room, pack what I have to pack and again leave the hotel.

I don't bother to check out, because I don't want to give Stuart that much notice that I am no longer here. Outside, I ask the bellman for a taxi, and wait with my head ducked while he summons one.

When it pulls up, I hand him a tip and slide in the back. The driver glances at me in the rearview mirror, his face bland of any recognition and says in heavily accented English, "Where to, *signore?*"

"The train station," I say and sit back.

10

Ty

NORMALLY, YOU WOULD have waited longer. Given her more time to absorb who you are, *what* you are to this firm. More time to draw the conclusion that you're a man who's worth the risk.

Normally, you let it be her idea. Even if you had to set her up a bit for it. You like for it to be her idea. It makes it way less complicated when things are over.

How can she blame you when she's the one who started it?

But this time, you don't want to wait. Maybe this thing with Lizzy has you so thrown for lack of a better word that you need some kind of reset to remind you that you're the one in control of your marriage, not Lizzy.

If she thinks she can do something like this without repercussion, she is wrong.

You're sitting at your desk, tapping a pencil against a white legal pad and working on your third cup of coffee when it occurs to you how incredibly stupid Lizzy is being. Did she forget that you're an attorney?

You take satisfaction in knowing that if you ever decide to end your marriage, you've already made sure that Lizzy will never be able to touch the majority of your assets.

You lean back in your chair, study the tan of your hands against your white shirt and wonder if she knows exactly how easy it would be for you to trade her in for a newer model.

Not that it hasn't occurred to you. It has. Many times.

Until this very moment, you've actually preferred things the way they are. Lizzy has been a constant in your life. Home base, if you will. And you have a short attention span. You get bored easily.

Maybe you're getting bored with Lizzy. The discontent you feel in her every evening when you get home from work. As if the life you share together is one she's merely tolerating.

The irony of it is like acid in your gut. She doesn't work. You do. She has all day to run. Read her books. Take care of the house. Tough life.

You can only imagine that there are plenty of women who would sign up for that lifestyle in a heartbeat.

And so, when the new associate knocks at your door and steps inside with the glow of twenty-something beautiful, you decide to test your theory.

11

Lizzy

I'VE SPENT THE entire day, another long, glorious self-indulgent day, meandering one street to another with no greater purpose than to see what lies at the end of the next street.

I have my iPad with me and sit at an outside table of a trattoria, reading the first book on my very long list of books to read while I'm here. I take my time with the most delicious salad I've ever eaten. The greens are fresh, as if someone just picked them from a kitchen garden. The olive oil is smooth and flavorful and made only an hour or so away, according to my polite and slightly flirtatious waiter.

Time has slowed for me here. I don't know if it's the fact that I don't have a cell phone attached to the palm of my hand, or that there's no painfully long to-do list prodding me toward completion. Or if it's that I am alone and I have nothing more to think about than what I will see next.

Whatever it is, I'm beginning to love this pace of life. I think of how quickly an ordinary day at home goes by, swallowed in bits and pieces by the everyday tasks that seem so necessary there.

Here, they don't seem necessary at all. Here, I wonder why the list of books that I would like to read has grown so long that I'm not sure I will actually finish them in my lifetime. Here, I read a book yesterday and will probably finish another today.

As much as I love to read, it has become something that I never quite get to.

Ty hates it when I read in the evenings. He can't understand why I would want to disappear into the pages of a book instead of talking to him. But then our talking isn't exactly talking. It's more me listening while he talks about his day, the cases he's working on. I nod, shake my head, agree, and sympathize.

I could resent this except that I will be the first one to admit that his days are usually far more interesting than mine. There's only so much I can say about the five-mile run I do each and every morning or the trip to the dry cleaners or post office. And so, at home, I've become an accomplished listener.

Across the square, an elderly woman sits on a bench with her back to me. She's facing a church, centered nearly with the front doors of the beautiful building. Its walls are washed with age, the golden color streaked and mottled, gracefully aged in the way of so many of the buildings in Florence.

Her dark hair, heavily streaked with gray, is anchored in

a bun at the nape of her neck. Her shoulders are perfectly straight, her posture that of a twenty-year-old runway model. I actually yearn for my camera. It's been so long since I've had that feeling that it startles me. To see something and recognize it as a moment that needs to be captured. It's a feeling I once loved completely.

I brought my camera along on the trip, but I've yet to take it out of the hotel room. Somewhere along the way, my photography had become a hobby that seemed to take a little too much of my attention. I believe those were Ty's exact words. This, when Kylie had been a teenager and required more of my time than she had as a toddler. There had been practices to drive her to after school, homework to help her with in the evenings.

It was one evening in particular when Kylie had been fourteen that I finally realized what Ty thought of my work. He'd gotten home late from the office. It was eleven or so. I had been in the dining room, sorting photos on the table for a show I had been asked to take part in the following month.

I'd been so intent on arranging the pictures that I hadn't noticed him standing in the doorway until he said, "Is there any purpose to what you're doing?"

Startled, I glanced up, meeting his gaze. It only took that one look in his eyes for me to know he had been drinking. He could never hide it. Something about alcohol unveiled a meanness in Ty that was otherwise never really present in him. I saw it clearly then and stepped back automatically.

"I'm working on these for the show at the museum on the fourth."

"Ah, yes, the one where we pay for a bunch of expensive frames to showcase your hobby."

It was a word he had certainly used before. A word I had come to dislike. In Ty's eyes, a label that made what I loved to do worthless. I guess that's the moment when I realized that's exactly how he saw it—a nice little pastime for me that kept me from being too unhappy when he came home at this hour of the night on a regular basis.

I hate to admit it, even now, because doing so casts me in a light I would rather not see myself in. A woman who started her adult life and her marriage with a clear identity, a very defined picture of who she wanted to be and how she saw herself getting there. The shoreline of that vision had really started to erode a long time ago. The waves small and so unobtrusive at first that I hadn't recognized the erosion. Over the years, the waves had continued to grow in size, eating away at my goals and ambitions until that moment in our dining room when I realized they no longer had any value at all, at least in the context of my marriage.

I can blame Ty for not realizing what his words did to me. I can blame him for thinking those thoughts in the first place. But I can't blame him for my own reaction to them. I can't blame him because I caved to them like a hollowed-out stretch of beach that finally redefines itself into the shape the ocean has forged for it.

I let myself be changed by Ty's point of view. I began to

see myself as he saw me. Spending too much time each day, too much energy, too much money on something that really didn't and wouldn't ever matter very much to anyone but me.

I backed out of the show, never discussing it with Ty, just removing it from our family calendar with the click of a delete button, gone. Insignificant enough not to be noticed or questioned by either my husband or daughter.

I don't know why I brought my camera on this trip. I haven't touched it in years. Maybe it was just one more outward sign of rebellion against Ty and his defaulting on our plans.

I study the back of the woman's head again; note the regal arch of her neck. I decide then and there that I have been missing out on too many beautiful moments. It doesn't matter if anyone else ever sees my pictures or not. They are for me, part of who I am and how I express my interpretation of what I see in this world. I've been silent too long.

~

I PAY MY CHECK and start walking back to the hotel, adamant now that I will not pass one more beautiful thing in this city without my camera to remember it by.

At the hotel, I step into the lobby, respond to the doorman's hope that I have enjoyed my day so far. We exchange pleasantries, his ability to express them in English far better than mine in Italian. He gives me a smile of approval at my willingness to try.

I head for the elevator, and out of the corner of my eye,

spot a tall, instantly familiar figure at the front desk. I stop before it even fully registers that I should keep going.

The desk clerk looks up at me and smiles, causing the man to glance over his shoulder. He's wearing a ball cap and dark sunglasses. Maybe that would fool a lot of people, but I am as certain of who he is as I am certain of my own name.

He meets my surely shocked gaze, and for what feels like an incredibly long stretch of seconds, we merely look at each other in silence, recognition clearly in place.

I feel my lips part with the intent of speaking. But something in his face stops me. He holds up a finger and says, "Wait. Please."

I actually glance over my shoulder to see if there is someone else behind me who he's talking to. His beautiful supermodel, perhaps. But there's no one there, just the elevator doors. And so, I stand waiting while he signs a piece of paper, hands it back to the clerk, picks up his bag and walks toward me. He nods his head at the elevator door and indicates for me to follow him.

I do, mute, even though I cannot begin to understand my own actions. He might be a rock star to the rest of the world, but I don't know him, and I'm not in the habit of following strangers into elevators, which is exactly what I do when the doors slide open, and he waits for me to step inside. He walks in behind me. The doors close.

"Hello," he says.

I try for the same, but the first attempt doesn't come out.

My "Hi" is hoarse at the edges, and there's a question mark at the end of it.

"You're still here," he says.

I try for a millisecond to figure out what that statement could possibly mean. So many things—and clearly none of them could be what I'm thinking. That he came here looking for me? Right.

"Yes," I say. "I am." I had forgotten to push the button for my second-floor room, and we glide to a stop on the fifth floor.

"Can you get off here for a moment?" he asks.

"Here?"

"Here," he says with a half-smile on his mouth.

"I . . . okay," I say, and follow him into the hallway.

He checks his key, glances at the numbered plaques on the wall indicating room direction and starts to the right.

"Ah," I say. "I really should get back to my room."

"Come inside for a second?" He holds up one hand as if to indicate harmlessness. "I'd rather not stand out here in the hallway."

I'm assuming by that he means he doesn't want to risk being recognized. Against the common sense I should certainly be exercising, I nod once and follow him silently to the end of the hallway where he opens double doors into a room quite unlike mine. I love my room, but this is something else altogether.

It occupies the front corner of the hotel. It's enormous, three sofas, several very cushy reading-type chairs, glass-pane doors that open out onto a terrace. Another set of doors lead into what must be the bedroom, and I deliberately avert my gaze from there, settling instead on the terrace.

He steps behind me to close the door. At the click of the lock, I jump a bit.

He looks at me as if he has noticed my unease and says, "I'm not stalking you."

I laugh a little. "Shouldn't I be the one stalking you?"

He shakes his head and says, "I didn't want you to think I followed you here with some evil purpose."

I try to frame a response at the same time I struggle to process exactly what he has said. But the two are in conflict, and what comes out is something between a laugh and a question. "You followed me here?"

He shrugs. "I kind of got out of Rome fast. When I got to the train station and the agent asked me where to, "Florence" just came out."

"Oh," I say, as if I understand now, when in actuality, I am even more confused. "Did something bad happen there?"

"Something normal," he says. "I'm trying to get away from normal for a little while."

I slide my hands down the skirt of my dress, a casual flimsy thing I had slipped on this morning with very little thought as to whether anyone would notice it or whether I would care if they did. I'm finding right now that I do care.

"Well, Florence, it really is an awesome place. Room service here is wonderful. American coffee is incredible." I break off there, realizing I sound like an infomercial with selling points that he's probably already aware of.

"All right then. I should be going. I actually came back to the hotel to get my camera before I finished my afternoon walking tour." Walking tour? Did I just say that? I sound like I'm at least eighty and traveling with the AARP.

"Where are you going?"

I feel my eyes widen at the question. I'm not exactly sure what I'm supposed to say. Is he asking out of polite interest? "I . . . to see David. You've been?"

"Yes," he says. "It's pretty amazing."

"Great. Well, I hope you—"

"Would you mind if I come along?"

Is he serious? There has to be a punchline in here somewhere. "Are you sure you want to do that?" I ask, grappling for reasons why this would be a bad idea. "I mean you might be spotted or something."

"I'm good," he says, "if you are."

"Ah, sure," I say. "I need to run downstairs and get my camera."

"Meet you in the lobby in five minutes?"

"Okay," I answer.

"See you then, Lizzy."

My hand is on the doorknob when he says my name, and I feel a shock of pleasure at the realization that he has remembered it. Just as quickly, I push that away and open the door, stepping out into the hallway.

I walk, more like run, to the elevator, press the button

repeatedly, as if that will make it arrive faster, until it glides to a stop. The doors swish open. I step inside and push the second-floor button, realizing I've been holding my breath since leaving his room. I let it out and then breathe in a deep pull of air.

What. Just. Happened?

I have no idea.

It's as absolutely unlikely as any fantasy scenario I might ever have created for myself.

At my room, I insert the key and push open the door, letting it slap closed behind me. I drop my purse onto the floor and press my palms to my cheeks, feeling the heat there.

I walk to the mirror across from the bed and look at myself. My wavy blonde hair has refused to remain in submission to the taming I gave it with my flat iron earlier this morning. Curls have reasserted themselves. My lips are as pink as my cheeks, and my eyes are a little glazed as proof that I'm having trouble believing the past ten minutes of my life.

Maybe he won't show up downstairs and will avoid running into me for the rest of his stay here.

This scenario makes sense. He seems like a nice enough guy, on the surface. Maybe he's trying not to hurt my feelings?

I go into the bathroom, reach for my toothbrush and brush my teeth until I no longer taste anything of the wonderful lunch I'd consumed an hour or so ago. I wrangle a brush through my hair, consider quickly plugging in the flat iron, glance at my watch and decide against it.

Of course, if I'm operating under the assumption that he's not going to actually show up, I should use the flatiron. What difference will it make if I'm a few minutes late?

Something inside me raises an unwelcome flag of hope, and I settle for the meager repair work of my hairbrush. I pull a tube of lipstick from my makeup bag, put some on, a subtle pink that brightens up my face and at the same time doesn't scream "I'm trying way too hard."

In the bedroom, I pull my camera bag from the drawer where I had stored it, slip it over my shoulder, grab my purse from the floor and head for the door.

The mirror stops me, beckons me to look. I do. And I'm not even sure I recognize who I see there looking back at me.

12

Ren

I WAIT FOR HER in the lobby of the hotel. I stand away from the door with my back turned to anyone coming in. I can see the square outside the window, and I watch the faces of other people laughing, talking, and eating. Two girls walk past, glance in at me. I pull my cap lower so that it's shadowing most of my face.

I look at my watch and realize it's been twenty minutes since I left my room. It occurs to me that maybe she won't come at all. Maybe she'll decide it was a crazy request on my part to ask to join her. And an even crazier response on her part to say that I could.

I think about that taxi ride out of Rome and how I'd had no clear picture of where I was going. Not until I'd actually boarded the train and watched the Italian countryside flowing by outside my window. I knew that I was in a bad place and that despite my protest to Stuart, I didn't really want to be alone. I wanted to be away. But not alone.

Alone is dangerous. Alone means I have to trust myself to leave that bottle in my leather case.

But sometimes, the temptation is so great that I can barely resist it. I know that what's in that bottle will bring oblivion, freedom from my thoughts. Sometimes, I crave it to the point that it is all I can think about.

On the train headed toward Florence, I had actually let myself play through the scenario. It would be so easy. I know how many pills I would have to take. I know how long before that amount would be likely to stop my heart. There's something I can only describe as comfort in this hidden knowledge. It's like a concealed weapon that I carry to protect myself from the bad stuff. Only the irony is that the bad stuff doesn't exist in the form of some lunatic hijacking my car or shooting me when I open the front door of my apartment. The bad stuff exists within me, and those pills are there to protect me from myself.

I hear footsteps behind me and turn to see Lizzy Harper stop several yards away from me, as if she's afraid to come closer. "Hey," I say.

"Hey," she replies back, clearly nervous.

We study each other for a second or two and then start to speak at the same time. I stop and let her speak first.

"Where do you want to go?" she asks.

"Wherever you were headed before I asked to come with you."

I see the questions in her face, and if I were a kinder person, I would say something to address them. But what explanation could I give her that wouldn't have her calling for the nearest psychiatrist?

And would I even blame her?

No. I wouldn't.

13

Lizzy

I AM WALKING down a street in Florence, Italy, with Ren Sawyer.

Granted, no one else would know he's Ren Sawyer.

Between the hat, the hoodie and the sunglasses, there's little chance of anyone recognizing him.

Clearly, that's his intent.

My stomach is so full of butterflies that I actually feel sick. I don't think I could make a coherent sentence come out of my mouth right now if my life depended on it.

My brain ends everything that starts to my lips, disqualifying it as inane, boring and not even remotely in the ballpark of anything a rock star would talk about.

As for me knowing what that might be, he could belong to another species. Which, actually, I guess he does, if you're dividing human beings into groups of like and unalike. People who live on similar planets. And people who don't.

I settle for a question. The most obvious one. "Why would you want to do this?"

"What?" he asks. And I can tell he's stalling.

"Come with me. Don't people like you have bodyguards, guided tours and stuff like that?"

"Sometimes," he says. "Although it gets old pretty fast."

"Just warning you, if a crowd gathers, and they get a little crazy, I'm probably not going to be much of a bodyguard."

He laughs at this, and when I glance at him, I really have to wonder if he's as surprised by the laughter as I am. I don't know what it is. I can't exactly put my finger on it, but there's this air about him that feels heavy and weighted, a curtain put in place to prevent others from seeing in.

His laugh is like a break in that curtain, through which I glimpse someone very different from the guy in all those pictures generated by my nosy Google search.

As quickly as it had appeared, the smile slips away again, and in its place, his former seriousness returns. "That's okay," he says, "I won't expect you to."

"Does it happen often?" I ask.

"What?"

"Things getting out of control when people recognize you."

"Not as much as it used to. I've gotten a little wiser."

"Ah," I say, as if I know exactly what he means when how could I possibly have any idea? "I was headed to the Accademia this afternoon. We can do something else if you'd rather—"

"No. I'd like to go."

We cover blocks and blocks then without speaking further, just walking, like two people who might know each other well enough not to need conversation, except that the explanation for our silence is something altogether different.

When I start to become uncomfortable with it, I pull my camera from its bag. I loop the strap around my neck; settle one hand on each side, remembering how much I love the feel of it.

"Nice," he says, looking at it.

"Thanks. I haven't used it in a while."

There's a stand up ahead operated by an older man with gray hair and a sun-lined face. His cart contains clear cups of deep red cherries. Next to that is a display of sliced coconut on ice. Enormous lemons line the top of the cart.

A sign says **Fresh-Squeeze Lemonade**.

His setup is small and simple, but utterly beautiful. My fingers itch to capture that beauty. I raise the camera, adjust the zoom and click. It is the first picture I've taken in years. Just like that, I feel a little piece of myself pop back into place. Like a joint that's been dislocated and then returned to its correct fit.

I don't think I realized how truly painful giving up my photography has been, until now when I once again feel the satisfaction it gives me.

I've snapped at least twenty shots when the man running the stand smiles at me and says, "You like?"

"Very much," I say.

"I am in one?" he says.

"Yes. Of course," I answer, smiling.

He doesn't pose, merely works at arranging the cups of fresh cherries at a better angle, adding slices of coconut to the ice. His white apron makes a nice offset against the vibrant colors of the fruit. He looks up once and smiles at me, his very white teeth gleaming against his sun-bronzed skin.

A customer walks up to buy a cup of cherries. The proprietor nods at me and says, "Thank you for me to be in photograph."

"No. Thank you," I say, stepping back. I bump into someone and turn suddenly, realizing that it is Ren, and at the same time becoming aware that I had truly forgotten he was standing there. I think he can see this in my face because I sense his surprise. I would imagine it's a response he doesn't get very often.

"You really love that," he says.

"Sorry, I didn't mean to take so long."

"Don't be. I enjoyed watching you."

My face goes instantly warm. I'm blushing. "Should we walk on?"

"Sure," he says, and we continue down the street.

Now that I've started, I can't seem to stop. Everywhere I look, I see something I want to capture.

A window displaying the most incredible pastries. Mounds of them on beautiful Tuscan-colored platters. Arranged so artfully in the window that it must be nearly impossible for anyone to walk by without going inside and buying one.

Pigeons squabble over a bread crust on the sidewalk.

Two old women walk along, arm in arm, ahead of us. They are the exact same height, are wearing similar coats, one in a bright pink, one a mint green. They chatter nonstop in Italian, one not quite completing a sentence before the other one starts the next.

I imagine that they are sisters, and they have talked this way all their lives. They laugh at something, and I click, catching the lines of amusement on their faces.

The Accademia is a thirty minute walk from the hotel. The only reason I know how to get there is because I walked by it yesterday and ducked inside to get a schedule of hours and things to see.

"Why have you been away from it?" he asks, so unexpectedly I have to think for a moment about what he is asking me.

"You said you've missed it," he adds. "Your photography."

The label is an obvious one, but I warm at the sound of it coming from him, at the same time remembering that I can't think of a time when Ty actually called it that. My pictures. My hobby. But not my photography.

"I guess it stopped seeming important in the big scheme of things," I say.

"To you?" he asks.

"No. It's always been important to me."

"Then unimportant to whom?"

"My husband," I say.

His gaze drops to my left hand and the wedding band on

my ring finger. I can see that it isn't the first time he's noticed it. I wonder if that's why he's here with me. Because I'm safe. Not a threat. Even though it's absolutely true, it's not what any woman wants to think of herself.

Reality is, however, reality.

According to my Google search, he is thirty-one. I'm thirty-eight with a college-age daughter. He's also a celebrity. A guy who dates supermodels, if I'm looking to acknowledge any further reasons why it would never occur to me to think that he has singled me out for anything remotely resembling attraction.

I actually feel a little embarrassed to find myself thinking along these lines. That's how ridiculous it seems.

"Why does he think it's unimportant?" Ren asks, pulling me back to the conversation.

I shrug. "I guess because it's not really something that contributes significantly to our lives."

"Does it contribute significantly to yours?"

I don't have to think about the answer. It springs up automatically, refusing to be tamped back. "Yes."

"Then it matters," he says, in a voice so full of conviction that I think how likely it is that no one ever disagrees with him.

"What I meant," I say, "is as a significant source of income."

"Things can be valuable even when there's no monetary value attached."

"But there's that word, compromise."

"In what way?"

"We make concessions. To get along with others. To make life go more smoothly. Even when we'd rather not."

"But that's when life begins to lose some of its shine, don't you think?" he asks.

"Are you saying you've never made any?"

"Concessions?"

I nod.

"I've made plenty."

"I imagine anyone who gets to where you are would have to make a few here and there."

"You have to be careful which ones you allow yourself to make. Some, you can adjust to. Others are game changers."

We're in front of the Accademia Gallery now. We walk inside and find the place to purchase tickets. I pay for mine first and then step aside and wait for him to get his.

At the entrance, we hand over our tickets and start down a hallway with offshoot rooms of priceless statues.

We step inside the first one. We separate at the center of the room. I wander left. He wanders right.

I begin reading the plaques denoting the artist and the year the work was created.

We intersect paths again at the end of one display. "Can you imagine creating something that would last this long? That people would travel from all over the world to see?" I ask.

"No," he says. "I really can't."

I glance at him. "Your work is kind of like that now. People come from all over the world to hear you."

"It's not the same," he says, "nowhere near the same."

"How so?"

He waves a hand at a statue in front of us. "This is lasting. Worthy. What I do isn't like that."

"It is to some people."

We walk on and continue looking, winding through another room full of marble statues, some of which sat outside for many years before being removed from the elements and housed here to prevent further damage.

We finally find our way to the gallery's most famous Michelangelo work: David.

I had imagined that it would be incredible, but anything I pictured in my mind doesn't come close to the real thing. First of all, he is more than seventeen feet tall, and so much wider, bigger than I had expected. The detail of his hands and feet is lifelike. I stare for a long time, studying every part, except for the part I can't look at with Ren Sawyer standing next to me.

Like the others around us, we're both quiet, simply taking it in.

"It doesn't seem possible, does it?" Ren says.

"No, it doesn't."

"I read that the enormous piece of stone he used to create David sat outside in a cathedral courtyard for twenty-five years when its original commission fell through. Michelangelo convinced authorities that he was the man for the job. Can you imagine the work involved—how long it would take? Not even counting that, how could he end up with this from a chunk of stone? It's nearly otherworldly."

"Yes," I say. I can come up with no better word for it. I think I could stand for hours, absorbing the magnificence of the creation. And even then, I'm not sure that would do it justice.

We wander away eventually, both of us notably reluctant. There are more exhibits to see. But somehow after David, it's hard to give the other works their fair share of credit.

It's late afternoon by the time we leave the gallery, and the sun has dropped enough that shadows dapple between the buildings.

I look at Ren and say, "Do you think Michelangelo had any way of knowing how people would see his work after he was gone?"

"I doubt that he could dream its effect would be this lasting."

"I hope he knew on some level the things that his creations have made people feel."

"Yeah, me too," he agrees.

We talk almost none for the rest of the walk back. I keep my camera in front of me, looking for the next shot. By the time we arrive in front of the hotel, I've taken at least a couple of hundred photos.

We walk through the main door and into the elevator. I can't deny feeling a little bit of a letdown that the afternoon is ending. But, of course, it has to, as I knew it would.

"Well," I say, righting my bag on my shoulder. "I hope you enjoy the rest of your visit in Florence."

"You too."

"Maybe we'll run into each other again," I say, even though I'm getting the feeling that he hopes that won't happen.

It's beginning to feel awkward so I decide not to ride up with him, making an excuse about needing to check for messages at the front desk. "So," I say, "see ya."

"See ya," he says and then quickly ducks into the elevator.

I feel a bit stunned at his departure, although I'd be the first to admit how ridiculous that is. Considering that the life I am currently on vacation from holds virtually no opportunities for anything like this to happen, I suppose I should just chalk it up to once in a lifetime—like being hit by a meteor.

If Kylie ever decides to have a conversation with me again, maybe I will tell her about it. Although I doubt that she would believe me. I walk over to the desk and check for messages with the receptionist, who hands me a piece of paper with a gold foil seal.

I thank her and wait until I'm in the elevator to open it.

Winn Everson asks that you call her at your earliest
convenience. Urgent.

I glance at my watch. Four-thirty p.m. here. It would be ten-thirty p.m. there.

My stomach drops at the tone of the note, and suddenly, real life comes crashing back in. I can't get to my room fast enough.

14

Lizzy

I IMMEDIATELY PICK up the telephone on the desk and tell the hotel operator that I would like to make a call. I give her Winn's cell number.

Possibly two minutes pass during which I can feel my heart thudding in my chest, and my imagination starts to run away with me. Finally, I hear a click and then a ring followed by Winn's not-quite-normal sounding, "Hello."

"Hey," I say. "I just got your message. Everything okay?"

"I'm sorry for leaving that. I hope it didn't scare you. But I really needed you to call me."

"I would have called you without the urgent part," I say, smiling a little in relief.

"So how is it? Italy?"

"Amazing. Beautiful."

"Just like you thought it would be?"

"Better, actually. Is everything all right, Winn?"

She sighs, long and miserable sounding.

"Winn, you're scaring me," I say.

"I shouldn't have called," she says, sounding suddenly doubtful.

"What is it?" I ask, really worried now.

"Jason was sick last night."

"Oh. I'm sorry. Is he all right?"

"He's fine. Just a stomach virus. Anyway, he wanted some ginger ale, and we didn't have any, so I drove to the store. It was like five o'clock this morning. I passed by your house, and there was a car in the driveway."

The last few words are rushed, as if she has to make herself get them out before she can change her mind. "And?"

"Ty's car was there too."

"Maybe Kylie came in with a friend," I start, not sure why Winn is making such a big deal out of this.

"It wasn't Kylie," Winn says.

"How do you know?"

A very long stretch of silence hangs between us before she says, "Because I recognized the car. It was Serena Billings."

I know the name as one of the recent hires at Ty's firm. I search for anything else that had been mentioned about her and can come up only with the fact that Ty had said she was uber smart. Had recently graduated from Yale and was considered a coup for the firm.

"Maybe they were working there last night, and she left her car for some reason." This explanation sounds ludicrous to me even as I'm voicing it. Ty has never brought an associate to our house to work before. So it's not exactly a habit I can draw on.

"There's more," Winn says.

Now the misery factor in her voice is amplified to a point where my stomach clenches in a knot.

"Winn. What is it?" Even as I ask the question, dread swoops down over me, and I know somehow that I do not want to hear her answer.

"I started not to tell you. You know what they say about everyone always wanting to kill the messenger."

"You're not the messenger. You're my best friend."

"I hope you'll still say that when I'm done."

"Winn, please!"

"Okay. I recognized her car because she recently joined the Junior League. We met after a luncheon at Chez Ma a couple of weeks ago. Her license plate is SOSUEME."

My stomach drops a few more floors, and this time I say the words through clenched teeth. "Just tell me, Winn."

"I went to the door. I rang the bell. Ty came downstairs. He was, let's say, shocked to see me. There was someone upstairs, Lizzy. I didn't see her, but I heard her. I asked him who it was, and he told me to mind my own f-word business. I told him I would, just as soon as I called you and let you know there was another woman in your bedroom."

I sit on the edge of the bed because I feel suddenly and completely sick. Like the time I had food poisoning and couldn't quit throwing up for twelve hours straight.

"I didn't want to tell you, Lizzy," Winn says, her voice breaking.

I can tell she's crying.

"But how could I not?" she asks.

My thoughts are spinning off in a dozen different directions, and I can't decide which one to grab first. How long has he been seeing her? Is this why he backed out of our trip? Why he worked so late? Have there been others?

"I'm sorry," Winn says. "I'm really so sorry."

I open my mouth to reply but nothing comes out.

"Are you angry with me?" she asks.

"Of course not," I manage. "Why would I be angry with you?"

"If I hadn't driven by there . . . if I hadn't stopped—"

"Then I would have just gone on being a fool, wouldn't I?" My voice breaks on the end of the question.

"You're not a fool, Lizzy. You trusted him. That's not the same thing."

"In this case it is." I try for a laugh, but it just comes out bent and unrecognizable.

"I'll come over there," Winn says.

"No, Winn. You just said Jason was sick."

"He'll be okay in a day or so, and I'll come."

"I'm fine," I say. "Really. Maybe it's not such a big surprise."

"It is to me."

If I'm honest, it is to me also. On this side of it, I don't know why. It's not as if our life together has actually been *together* for a very long time. It didn't happen overnight, but

93

gradually, so that it was hard to notice the extent of it on a daily basis. And still, I had not guessed this. I would not have guessed this. Naïve fool that I am.

"Maybe this is the first time, Lizzy."

"Please, don't, Winn."

"You don't know for sure."

"We haven't slept together in over a year."

"What?" Winn finally asks, shocked.

The silence is heavy, as if we're in a locked room and a naked person has just dropped out of the air to stand between us.

Winn mumbles, "Maybe that's why he—"

"Don't even go there," I say quickly. "Abstinence wasn't my choice."

"*He* hasn't wanted to?"

I feel suddenly ashamed because how could anyone think that I wasn't in some way to blame for it? "I had hoped this trip would be a renewal for us." A laugh bubbles up out of me, but then morphs into a sob. Once the tears start, I can't stop them. I can't even speak.

"Lizzy," Winn says. "Let me come over there."

I'm tempted. I am so tempted. Because more than anything, I want someone to lean on, to cry against. Someone who knows me. Who understands exactly what this is doing to me.

At the same time, I cannot stand the thought of her seeing me like this, witnessing firsthand the demolition of my self-respect from the inside out. Maybe in a while when I've picked up some of the pieces and started to put myself together again. Only right now, staring up at the ceiling of this room for which I had declared unyielding love just this morning, I cannot begin to imagine when that will be.

"Give me a bit, Winn," I say, struggling to make my voice even and convincing. "I'll call you in a couple of days, okay?"

"You don't need to be alone right now, Lizzy."

"Actually," I say, "that is exactly what I need. Be good," I add, and hang up.

I stand, slowly, carefully, as if my bones have become fragile and might break at any unexpected move. I take off all my clothes and get in the shower. It's the only place I can think of to go where my tears will instantly be washed away, and no one can hear me cry.

15

Ty

DAMN. NOSY. BITCH.

You pace the kitchen one end to the other. You rake a hand through your hair and tell yourself to calm down.

What are the frigging odds of Winn showing up at the front door at five o'clock in the morning?

Okay, so maybe you had been a little careless. Letting Serena drive here, leave her car parked out front.

But then both of you had been a little too drunk to think that part through, which isn't at all like you. You like to cover the bases. Look ahead for the pitfalls. Anticipate instead of decimate.

This could definitely fall under the category of decimation.

You almost wonder if Winn planned the whole thing.

You've suspected more than once that she had doubts

about you. Although there was a time when you were fairly sure you could have had her if you'd wanted her.

But you didn't, and she had known it.

And it looks like she's finally found a chance to pay you back.

You had seen it in her eyes just before she turned away from the front door and stalked back to her car, all haughty superiority.

You'd really love taking her down a peg or two. In fact, you're sure if you dig around a little, you can find some interesting facts about her own husband that you're pretty sure she doesn't have a clue about.

But that will save for later. Right now, you need a plan for how to fix this with Lizzy. If and when your marriage ends, it will be on your terms, at your instigation, not because Lizzy's busybody friend sees fit to make it happen.

You force yourself to put aside your anger to focus solely on what is most likely to prevent Lizzy from believing Winn's side of this story.

And then it occurs to you. You'll do what she'd wanted you to do all along.

16

Ren

IT'S AFTER EIGHT p.m. when I wake up. I hadn't really meant to fall asleep, but it seems to hit me like that these days. This utter fatigue that makes me feel like I have no other choice but to sleep.

I'm starving. I could order room service, but somehow, finding a place outside the hotel sounds more appealing.

I take a shower, get dressed and then grab a book from my suitcase before leaving the room. I'm in the elevator, headed for the lobby when I think about her.

I wonder if she's had dinner. I'm tempted to get off on the second floor, knock at her door and see if she wants to go with me.

It's not a good idea though. I know it. I knew it this afternoon when we got back from the museum. Something told me then that the smart move would be for me to at least imply that we probably wouldn't see each other again.

She's married. I'm a mess. We're not exactly the likeliest of friends.

But I enjoyed her company. That hasn't been true of anyone in my life for a very long time.

Not since my brother, Colby, in fact.

I resist pushing the second-floor button, step out into the lobby when the doors open. I walk by the front desk, glance at the keys lined up behind the clerk and notice that hers is gone, which means she's in her room.

I head for the door, and then, on impulse, turn back and walk over to the table where a house phone sits. I pick up the receiver and dial her room number. The line buzzes over and over again with no answer. I hang up, thinking maybe she forgot to leave the key when she went out.

I walk into the street, deciding to go right. I pull my baseball cap down lower over my eyes since wearing sunglasses at night would make me stand out more than blend in. I don't have to go far to find the kind of place I'm looking for. Small. Family run. Everything on the menu homemade.

I ask for the back corner of the restaurant where I can see but not be seen so easily. There's a candle on the table. I read my book, drink some really good wine and eat a large bowl of tagliolini tossed with rosemary and olive oil.

The story is good. I actually lose myself in it for a couple of hours. No one looks twice at me, including the young waitress who takes my order and brings my food. Anonymity is something I haven't felt in a good while. It's like stepping outside into the cool spring air after being inside all winter.

I walk back to the hotel with the book tucked under my arm, feeling full from the great meal, but somehow lighter from the stretch of time during which I'd gotten lost in a story.

In the lobby, I see that Lizzy's key is still not on its hook. Which means she could either be back or still out. This time, I ignore my common sense and push the button for the second floor. I get out and walk to her door without examining my reasons for doing so too closely.

I knock, but there's no answer. I wait thirty seconds or so and then turn to go. I hear something though that makes me stop and listen. It sounds like crying. And it's definitely coming from her room. Given that she didn't answer, it's clear she doesn't want company. We don't know each other well enough for me to think I have any right to ask her what's wrong. But I can't deny being concerned, so I knock again.

This time, I call out her name in a low voice. Silence now but she still doesn't answer. "Lizzy? It's me. Ren. Are you all right?"

"Yes," she says through the door. "I'm fine. Thanks. Goodnight."

"Goodnight," I say, reluctant, and yet what else, really, can I do?

I walk back to the elevator, get inside but just before pushing the button, step back out again. I stop in front of her door, and that's when I hear the crying again. "Lizzy? You're not all right. Will you please open the door?"

"I'm fine."

I stand for a moment, aware that I'm about to cross a line I have no right to cross. This has all kinds of red flags waving in front of me. For some reason, I ignore them. "If you don't let me in, I'm going to go downstairs and tell them I think something is wrong. Then you'll not only have me to contend with, but them as well."

A full two minutes pass before I hear her unlatch the chain. She pulls it open, barely wide enough to peer around it and say, "I'm okay. Thank you for your concern, but—"

I push just hard enough to get her to step back and let me in. I see the surprise on her face. Maybe I've surprised myself a little too. I close the door and stand looking at her. "What happened?" I ask.

"Nothing," she says.

"Nothing wouldn't make you look like you've been crying for hours."

She bites her lower lip and looks as if she's going to cry again despite an obvious resolve not to.

"Have you had dinner?"

She shakes her head. "I'm not hungry."

I notice then that she's wearing the hotel's white cotton robe. She doesn't appear to be wearing anything under it. She notices me noticing it and steps back, wrapping her arms around her waist.

"Can you just go, Ren? Please." She walks to the bathroom

and closes the door. I sit down on the sofa in one corner of the room and wait for her to come back out.

When she returns, she does not look happy to see that I'm still here. She's dressed in regular clothes now, a skinny white skirt and a light blue fitted T-shirt. I actually feel a little disappointed by this.

"You don't need to stay," she says.

"Even if I believed you, I'd rather hang out here a while than go back to my room."

"Why?" she asks.

"I don't know. It seems awfully quiet."

"I guess you are used to a lot of noise, aren't you?"

The assertion is not a compliment, and for the first time, I wonder what she really thinks of what I do.

"I'm sorry," she says. "I'm really not fit for company right now."

"That's okay," I say. "We can just hang. I'll read, and you do whatever you need to do."

She stares at me for several long seconds, and says, "You're not going to leave, are you?"

"I can't hear you," I say, looking at the pages of my book. "I'm reading."

I feel her wanting to say something. But, as if she doesn't have the energy, she goes over to the bed and lies on her side, not facing me.

Now that she can't see me, I do look at her. It's easy to see that this isn't the woman I went to see David with this afternoon. That woman seemed as if she wanted to absorb every speck of beauty around her. It had beckoned something inside me to do the same. I don't know, maybe that's why I left her in the lobby, not intending to see her again. No one has made me feel anything remotely like that for a very long time.

But this woman is broken.

I really don't need to get involved with broken.

Still, I get up from the sofa and walk around to face her. Her eyes are closed, and I can tell she knows I'm there, but refuses to look at me.

I squat down at the side of the bed, brush the back of my fingers across her cheeks, and say, "Whatever it is, it'll be okay again."

She opens her eyes and looks at me. Tears brim over and spill down her face. She bites her lower lip to keep from crying outright. That's when I stand, scoot her over and sit beside her. I slip my arms under hers, pull her halfway up to a sitting position, and I just hold her. It seems like that's what she needs, and I'm here. We're virtual strangers, and even though I can't explain why, I don't want to be anywhere else.

17

Kylie

SHE SHOULD HAVE quit before that last shot.

Kylie knows her limits where alcohol is concerned, but Peyton has a way of making her agree that "just one more" won't hurt. When actually, Kylie knows that it will hurt tomorrow morning when she has to get up for class and sit through an English lecture with pounding temples.

The bar is Charlottesville's most popular hangout for college kids. There are plenty of others in town, but Kylie and Peyton like this one because they have a live band every night of the week.

Tonight, alternative rockers have attracted a whole gaggle of freshmen girls to the front of the stage. The majority of them are looking at the lead singer as if they're all three year olds being introduced to their first lollipop.

She squints a little to bring him into better focus.

So maybe he's a nine on a scale of ten. But he knows it, so in her estimation, that drops him a point or two.

The music is loud. The beat of the drum and bass guitar pound in unison with her pulse.

He catches her stare, and Kylie feels the jolt of electricity surge through her. Peyton walks up just then and says, "You go for it, girl."

Kylie breaks the look, glancing at her friend with a no-idea-what-you're-talking-about smile. "You've had too much tequila," she says.

"Define too much."

"Judgment-impaired."

"My judgment is working just fine, and it looks as if yours is too. At the next set break, why don't you go say hello?"

"Like I could do that," Kylie says.

"Why couldn't you do that? He just gave you the look, an open invitation."

Kylie wants to deny it, and as much as she hates to admit it, Peyton is usually right where these things are concerned.

The band ends the song, and the crowd of girls up front goes wild, clapping and cheering, screaming the lead singer's name. "Jack! Jack! Jack!"

"Jack and Kylie," Peyton teases.

"Shut up," Kylie says. But she's thinking he is awfully cute. And she does have a thing for singers.

The band starts up the next song, and it's a minute or more before the girls up front lower their screaming enough that it becomes recognizable. It might be Kylie's favorite song ever: "Whatever the Wait" by Temporal.

She closes her eyes and soaks up the words. His voice is not nearly as good as Ren Sawyer's, but he holds his own with the melody, and when Kylie opens her eyes to find him staring at her again, she decides that maybe Peyton is right.

She'll hang around for a bit after the show.

18

Lizzy

MY EYES OPEN to a slit of light coming through the curtain of my room. It takes me a moment to remember where I am. Florence. And how I fell asleep. Ren.

He's sitting up with his back against the headboard. My head is on his chest, his wide, well-muscled chest. My left arm is draped across his legs. I sense that he is awake, and I remain frozen for a moment, trying to decide if I am ready to confront how we both fell asleep last night.

"Good morning," he says.

I close my eyes again, squeeze them shut tight, as if that will make all of this go away when I open them again. It does not, however, and I manage a lowly murmured, "Good morning."

It's then that I catapult myself up and off the bed. Once my feet hit the floor, I have a little trouble righting myself and sway like a sapling in a March wind. He reaches out, takes my hand to steady me and says, "Whoa, there."

I back up a few steps, suddenly and overwhelmingly aware that I haven't yet brushed my teeth and say, "I'm not exactly sure what happened here."

"Just wanted to make you stop crying. That's all."

"Thank you," I say, unable to imagine how that begins to cover it.

"You're welcome." He stands then and walks to the door. "I'm going up to take a shower. See you later?"

"Yeah," I say. "Later."

I wait for the door to click shut behind him and then force myself into my own shower where I lean against the marble wall, letting the spray pound my face. I try to process everything that happened last night, one strand at a time. But my thoughts keep getting knotted up like the ear buds I use for running and am forever untangling.

Ty doesn't love me anymore.

This one thought manages to sort itself out from the pile. I hang on it, letting its full meaning settle into me. I wait for the tears to come again, but this morning, they don't. I feel like a well that has been drained, and now I'm just empty.

It really should be no surprise that Ty is having an affair. From here, the signs are pretty clear. How little time we spent together. How distant we have become with each other. How rarely he touches me.

But it is a surprise. And I just feel foolish. Foolish for giving him my complete and total trust. Foolish for never questioning the why behind all the hours he works. Late nights and weekends spent at the office.

In my defense, the guy I married was deserving of my trust. I don't know at what point along the way he became the man he currently is, the one who does not deserve it. And I don't suppose that it really matters anymore. I think of how lonely I've been the last couple of years, with Kylie no longer in the house as a diversion. How utterly alone I have felt at times. And I cannot begin to even imagine how gullible I am in his eyes.

Believing myself still married to the same man who had proposed to me in the delivery room right before the birth of our child. Who'd had a pastor waiting outside the double swing doors? And at my "Yes," quickly urged him in to perform the ceremony before Kylie arrived.

I don't know what happened to that boy or how I lost him. But I have, and he is gone.

~

I HEAR A KNOCK as I'm getting out of the shower. I reach for a robe, slip it on and open the door.

A bellman hands me an envelope. "A fax for you, Signora."

He leaves with a polite nod, and I close the door, pulling the paper out and unfolding it.

The fax is on Ty's law firm stationery and written in his handwriting.

Arriving in Florence at 11:30 a.m.
I will meet you at the hotel. We need to talk.

Ty

I glance at my watch. It's just after nine. I read the message again. He will be here in two-and-a-half hours. Here in this hotel where I had thought we would celebrate our anniversary together. Now he's coming. And all it took was me finding out he's having an affair.

I ball up the piece of paper and drop it in the trashcan.

I pick up the phone and ask the front desk for the number of the closest rental car agency. They give it to me, and I dial immediately. The man who answers speaks good English, and within five minutes, he has arranged for me to pick up a car at their main office ten blocks from the hotel.

I pull my suitcase out of the closet and methodically begin to put in my clothes. In the bathroom, I collect all my toiletries, pack them up in their clear makeup bag and then toss that in the suitcase as well.

I'm dressed with my hand on the doorknob when a knock sounds from the other side. A little frantic, I glance through the peephole, afraid that Ty will have somehow managed to get here earlier than his fax indicated.

But it's not Ty standing in the hallway. It's Ren. I open the door, and he stares at me for a moment, clearly surprised.

"Where are you going?"

"I'm, ah, leaving."

"Leaving Florence or leaving Italy?" His voice is soft and surprised.

"Leaving Florence."

"Where are you headed?"

For a moment, I'm not sure how to answer. "I just decided to get out and see some of the countryside."

"Are you coming back?"

"No. I don't expect I'll be coming back here." I hesitate, glance away and then meet his questioning gaze again. "It was really nice meeting you, Ren. And thank you for last night. For being kind. For everything, actually."

I start through the doorway, pulling my suitcase out into the hall.

He stops me with a hand on my shoulder. "This wasn't planned, was it?"

I consider lying, but what would be the point? As ridiculous as it sounds, it's as if he can see through my walls and already knows what I'm thinking. "No," I say. "Kind of unexpected."

"And I'm guessing it has something to do with last night?"

This time I don't answer because I don't trust myself to do so without crying again.

We're quiet for a string of weighted moments. Before I can put together an answer, he breaks the silence.

"Would it be all right if I come with you?"

I blink, shake my head, sure I must have misheard him. "What?"

"I'll come with you." This time, there's no question in his voice.

"Ren. You really don't have to . . . I'm fine. You're very sweet."

He laughs at this, and I'm guessing sweet is something he isn't called very often. "I don't have any real schedule, so—"

"So you're just going to get in a car and drive around Italy with me?"

He shrugs. "Why not?"

I am not an unintelligent woman, and I'm fully aware this would be a moment where using my intelligence might be highly recommended. My marriage has just caved in around me. I have an either furious or contrite husband about to arrive in this city, and I do not need to be dragging a far-too-good-looking-for-my-own-good rock star into the middle of all of it.

Of course, I'm not exactly dragging him, but even so, I try one more time. "I really don't think you want to get in the middle of everything I have going on right now. It's probably best if I just head out of here alone and find somewhere quiet to think for a bit."

"Probably," he agrees. "But I still want to come. Give me ten minutes, and I'll meet you in the lobby."

"Seriously?" I say.

"Seriously."

I shake my head, trying to find a convincing protest. "This is crazy. People don't do things like this."

"I admit it's a departure for me," he says, with notable irony.

"Then why?"

He shrugs. "Maybe the better question is why not?"

19

Lizzy

THE RENTAL IS A FIAT. I'm driving. Ren is in the passenger seat, his six-three frame positioned accordion style with his knees pressed against the dash. He's wearing sunglasses and a baseball cap, which I noticed him pulling a little lower over his face when the woman at the car rental agency kept checking him out.

I reach under my seat for the map and hand it to him. "Can you navigate?"

He looks at it as if it's some hundred-year-old relic I've dug up from a deep hole. "Ah, maybe. Where are we going?"

"There's a little town I circled not too far from Florence. Could you find it?"

He opens the map. One edge touches the windshield to his right, the other landing midway across the steering wheel, taking up more than half the car's interior. He finds Florence, places his thumb there and with the other hand locates my circled area. He gives me the first road name to look for. We drive in silence for a few minutes, keeping an eye out for the sign. He spots it, just as I'm zipping past.

I head for the next intersection, make a controlled left-hand turn and then whip back onto the road, going back to the one we missed. We wait at a very long stoplight and then finally cross the highway and hit the onramp without missing it this time.

We stay on this road for twenty miles or so before Ren looks at the map and says, "Uh-oh."

"What?"

"I think we were supposed to turn back there."

I take the next exit, swing the car around again and find the road.

We've missed the third one, when Ren looks at me and says, "How attached are you to this map?"

"We have to have a map," I say.

He pulls his phone from his pocket, taps an app, types in something and hits search. Three seconds, and it's there on the screen, a computerized voice telling us what to do next.

"Okay," I say, halfway rolling my eyes, "if you can't read a map."

He balls it up and tucks it under the seat. "Unnecessary suffering."

"Some things are better in the old version," I say.

"Like?"

"Coke in glass bottles."

"Agreed," he says, tipping his head.

"Journey, before Steve Perry left."

"Debatable."

"Harry Potter. Books were better than the movies."

"Won't argue."

I consider my next answer and then, "Paper bags at the grocery store instead of plastic."

"Yep. Still not giving you maps."

The GPS voice pipes up just then. "One quarter mile ahead, stay right."

He smiles, but I pretend not to see it.

It's two o'clock when we arrive in the charming hillside Tuscan town.

I pull into a parking space and say, "I kind of wanted to walk around and see what's here. If you want to check things out on your own, that's fine."

"I'm good to tag along," he says.

"Okay," I say, still not sure I have any idea why he wants to be here. We get out of the car, the doors slapping closed behind us. I hit the remote lock, then remember my camera and go back for it.

The streets are cobblestone and worn smooth from centuries of people, just like us, walking through on days just like this. Small shops occupy either side of the street, and I wander in and out looking at original watercolors and oils in vivid colors.

Ren does his own thing. Sometimes, we're in the same store, sometimes not. At the top of the street, a wine store sits on the right. I walk in; peruse the many labels, some of which are very expensive. At the back of the store, an open entryway leads to a terrace overlooking a Tuscan valley that stretches out in front of me for miles. It is absolutely breathtaking.

I lean against the wall, take out my camera and begin shooting frame after frame after frame. With each one, I feel that old feeling of having struck gold, finding something uniquely lovely to capture within my lens. I hear him walk up behind me. It startles me to realize I know the sound of his walk. It hasn't registered until now. But it's a little unsettling to think I've already absorbed the details of him in this way.

He stops beside me and says, "Incredible."

"It is," I say.

He sits on the wall, swings his legs around to the other side.

"You might fall," I say, looking down at the twenty-foot drop below us.

"Or I might not," he says.

I'm not sure I agree with his logic, but the view is too inspiring to resist, so I sit and swing my legs over as well. I lift my camera, adjust the zoom and take some more pictures. "I love the trees here," I say.

"Which ones?"

I point at the tall, shapely rows lining a long pea gravel drive in the distance.

"Italian cypress," he says.

"Yes."

He points to a spot near the center of our view. "That looks like a grove of olive trees."

I refocus my camera on one of them, its silvery green leaves glinting in the sunlight. The houses in the valley have clay tile roofs, their stucco walls are earthy shades of gold and terra-cotta. "Looking at this makes me wish I could paint," I say.

"I'd like to see some of your pictures," he says, his palms planted on the wall, his gaze fixed on the scene in front of us.

I decide not to answer him because if he's just saying it to be polite, I don't want him to feel obligated at some point to stand and leaf through hundreds of my pictures.

"Does that make you uncomfortable?"

"No, I just—"

"I wouldn't say it if I didn't mean it."

"Okay," I agree, and decide I need to get better at taking compliments.

"So what's the plan for tonight? Please tell me we're not sleeping in the car."

I actually smile at the thought of it. "That might be a little more possible for me than you. I was thinking I'd just find a place."

He studies me for a moment and then says, "Want to tell me why you had to get out of Florence so fast?"

"No," I say softly.

"Jewel heist?"

"Me?"

He lifts his shoulders in a questioning shrug.

I laugh, surprising myself. "No."

"You're CIA?"

This time my laugh is more of a snort. I clamp a hand over my mouth. "Stop."

He keeps his gaze on the valley in front of us, his tone serious now. "I'm assuming it had something to do with last night?"

"Can we not go there?"

"We cannot," he says and turns around on the wall to stand. "I'm going to buy a bottle of that great wine out there and ask the person up front for a hotel recommendation."

I look over my shoulder to watch him go, and it's hard not to notice his appeal. The dark, slightly wavy hair sticking out from under his ball cap, his wide shoulders and that loose, self-assured walk.

He goes over to one of the wine cases and stands reading the label. I notice a woman watching him from a corner of the store. Her eyes convey clear interest. I make myself look away because it's none of my business who looks at him. I start taking pictures again but seem to have lost my focus.

I climb off the wall and walk back inside the store where Ren is now at the register paying for two bottles of wine. The pretty Italian cashier states the price in Euros, and I blink, wondering if I misheard.

Ren hands her a credit card and says, "Can you recommend a hotel somewhere in the area?"

She looks up at him, then glances at me, smiles and says, "Expensive or not?"

"Interesting," he says.

"Villa Florentine. It is four kilometers from here. It is a home that belonged to one of the most well-known families in the area. Five years ago, it was made into a luxury hotel. Many things to do there."

"Okay," Ren says. "Thank you." He picks up the two bottles of wine. We head out of the store and start back down the street toward the car.

"Did you buy the vineyard or just those two bottles?" I ask.

He gives me a half-smile. "I like good wine. And I'm willing to share."

"All right then," I say.

20

Ren

I FIND THE Villa Florentine on the GPS, and it takes us about ten minutes to get there. We turn off the main road onto a pea-gravel drive lined with cypress trees. I realize it's one of the houses we saw from the wall at the wine store.

"Wow," Lizzy says, looking up through the windshield at the tall trees. "If I were a painter, I'd have to pull over and capture this. Even if it took me a month."

"You can do that with your camera."

"Would you mind?"

"Of course not."

She pulls the car over, gets out and grabs her camera bag from the tiny back seat. I wait while she aims her lens in every direction at various angles. I see her nearly instant absorption and the way she connects with what she sees. The longer

I watch her, the more I realize how much I am enjoying observing her without her self-conscious awareness.

She walks back to the car a few minutes later with a look of chagrin. "Sorry," she says. "I didn't mean to overdo it."

"I like your passion for it," I say.

She looks instantly surprised by this. "Thanks," she says softly, noticeably avoiding my eyes, as if she thinks I'm just being polite.

I reach over and touch her arm. "Really."

She meets my gaze then, confusion clear on her face. She battles with it for a moment, and then releasing a breath, says, "Thank you."

She pulls back onto the road, the driveway leading up to the villa that is now a hotel a half-mile or so long. It appears to be a real find. The villa is enormous, its finish that weathered-gold so popular in the area, the clay tile roof a perfect complement. Large old trees lay claim to the length of time the villa and its adornments have occupied the space.

I had called ahead to make sure two rooms were available. They are expecting us when we arrive at the front desk.

The woman who greets us has long, black hair. Her earrings are the big loopy kind, and her smile is bright and welcoming. "We were able to get you adjoining rooms. I hope this is all right?"

There is an awkward pause of silence before Lizzy and I answer in unison without looking at each other, "Yes, that's fine."

"Wonderful," she says, taking a set of keys from the wall behind the desk. "I will show you."

We follow her through the lobby and up a very wide, winding set of travertine stairs to the second floor. The rooms are in the middle of the long hallway. She opens the first door, and I wave Lizzy inside. The woman then opens the other door, and I thank her and hand her a tip.

"*Grazie.* If you need anything at all, call the front desk. Please. Enjoy your stay."

I lift my suitcase onto the luggage rack, unzip it and pull out a few things, including the leather shaving case at the bottom. I take it into the bathroom and open it. It's only in seeing the bottle tucked into one corner that makes me realize I haven't been thinking about it.

I plant my palms on the edge of the sink, look at myself in the mirror. For a little over a day now, I haven't felt the leaden boulder on my chest. The realization comes with a jolt of surprise. Is that why I talked Lizzy into letting me come along with her?

Whether I was aware of it at the time or not, I guess it is. I have no idea how or why. But something about her makes something in me remember who I used to be.

I take a shower. About an hour after we've arrived, I carry one of the bottles of red wine and two glasses to Lizzy's door and knock. I hear something drop, a yip that sounds very much like a curse. She opens the door, her hair still poufy from the blow dryer. She's rubbing the top of her foot with one hand.

"What happened?" I ask.

"Hazards of beautification. I dropped the flat iron on my foot."

I try not to smile. "Did it burn you?"

"No. I'm fine. Just not very good with beauty tools."

"I would argue that you don't need them."

Her eyes widen, and I again watch her struggle with the question of whether I am serious or joking.

She quickly changes the subject with, "According to the information in the room, there's a great-sounding restaurant downstairs."

"Want to start this bottle of wine and then eat there?"

"Sure. My terrace?"

"Following you."

"I'll be right there," she says and ducks into the bathroom.

I walk outside, enjoying the cool night air and the quietness of the countryside beyond the hotel. I love the peacefulness here. The fact that life doesn't feel as if it's zooming by too fast to even begin to take it all in. I think of how I used to thrive on doing as much, getting as much, being as much as I possibly could. It's as if a switch has been flipped in me, and I wonder how I ever wanted any of that life.

When Lizzy comes out, her hair is straight and smooth. I notice, not for the first time, that the color is like twists of peanut butter and caramel. It's both thick and silky, and I feel a sudden and overwhelming need to run my fingers through it.

As a diversion, I pull the wine corkscrew from my back pocket, the cork making a satisfying pop. I run the bottle under my nose and let her do the same.

"Um," she says. "I don't know very much about wine, but that smells really good."

I pick up a glass from the wrought-iron table between us, fill it halfway and hand it to her. I then pour myself one, set the bottle down and walk to the wall that looks out over a softly lit pool below us.

She raises her glass. "To Tuscany," she says.

"To Tuscany."

She takes a sip, considers it for a moment and then says, "That is amazing. How did you know to pick this one?"

"From my last visit and doing a little reading."

"You read a lot."

I tip my head. "That's what I did instead of going to college. We got started with the band after high school. I tried to do both, but it didn't work out too well."

"I'd like to say I know a good bit about your band, but I'm afraid I really don't."

"I'm relieved to hear it."

She smiles and says, "Got a lot of skeletons in that closet, huh?"

"A few."

"Want to bring any of them out?"

"No," I say. "Definitely not."

She sits in one of the chairs close to the wall, crosses her legs, rests her elbows on her knees and takes another sip of the wine. I pull up the other chair and sit next to her. For several long minutes, we don't say anything. We just sit, sipping wine and looking out at the incredible view in front of us.

When I speak, it's to admit, "There hasn't been anyone in my life in a very long time I can sit beside and not feel obligated to make conversation, even when there's nothing meaningful about it."

She looks at me and says, "Thanks."

"It's really easy to be around you."

"I'm a fairly normal girl," she says, and her smile seems a little forced.

"I don't think you're normal at all," I say, realizing there are any number of ways she could take that assertion. But she seems to take it in the way I meant it and smiles at me. I don't know whether it's the wine or attraction that sends the surge of warmth through my chest.

I'm pretty sure wisdom would dictate chalking it up to the wine.

21

Lizzy

WE FINISH THE bottle in the room before heading downstairs to the restaurant. Ren asks for a table in the far corner, and although he doesn't say it, I'm sure it's to stay out of the center of things. I've noticed the way he never quite meets gazes with people, glancing away before they have a chance to make eye contact. He's done it three times so far since we sat down at the table.

"Does it get old?" I ask.

He glances up. "What?"

"The constant ducking and hiding in plain sight."

He looks a little surprised by the question, but then says, "It didn't always. Not at first. But after the novelty of having people chase you down the street wears off, it stops seeming like such a great thing. I asked for it though. Every bit of it."

"What do you mean?"

"I ran after the fame thing full blast, no ifs, ands or buts. I wanted it."

"It wasn't what you thought it would be?" I ask.

"Things are rarely what they appear on the surface," he says. "Fame, least of all."

I consider this and then ask, "What's the worst experience you've ever had that came from being famous?"

Without hesitating, he says, "A naked woman hiding in the closet of my hotel room until I got in bed, and she decided to join me."

I laugh. I can't help it. "Was she pretty at least?"

"Pretty, I didn't notice so much. Aggressive, I noticed."

"Some guys wouldn't consider that such a bad thing."

"In this case, bad thing," he says.

"So what's the best thing you've ever had happen because of being famous?"

"Putting on a private show for a little boy who was dying of cancer," he answers without hesitating. "He got an email through to my manager and asked if we could play his sister's birthday party at his house. He wasn't asking for him. He wanted to give her a gift he thought she would always remember him by."

I absorb what he just said. Tears instantly spring to my eyes at the image. "That's as good a reason to be famous as any I can think of. To be able to do something like that for someone is pretty amazing."

"It wasn't much, believe me."

"To both of them, I'm sure it was the world."

He looks down, and I can see he isn't comfortable with the praise.

"You don't act like you're famous," I say.

He laughs a short laugh. "How am I supposed to act?"

"I don't know. Like you own the universe or something. Don't most celebrities have big egos?"

He shrugs. "Sometimes, I wonder if it's actually the opposite. If there's not some deep down need for validation inside those of us who go for the lime light. Like maybe we need proof that other people see us as mattering."

It is not what I expected him to say, not by a long shot. "I thought a person would never be able to get up in front of thousands of people the way you do without having some pretty extreme confidence."

"We started out playing in the smallest places a band could actually play in and still legitimately call it a gig. I cut my performance teeth on singing in front of people who really could have cared less whether I was up on stage or not. That worked to my advantage, I think. I got to the point where I could just sing without thinking about who was listening and how I might fall short in their eyes because mostly they were ignoring me."

He's quiet for a stretch of moments, to the point where I wonder if I've asked a question that is too personal.

When he answers, his voice is low and distant. "No. It was actually my brother and me. We started taking guitar lessons when I was nine, and he was eight. That was our dream—to put together a band."

"Does he also sing?" I ask.

"He didn't. No, he played lead guitar."

I notice the past tense and wonder what I've stumbled into.

"He died a few years ago," Ren says in a low voice.

"Oh. I'm so sorry. I didn't realize."

"It's okay. My not talking about it isn't going to bring him back."

And with the statement, I can feel that something is different. Closed off in him like a vault door that shuts up tight things ordinary people should not have access to.

~

THE RESTAURANT IS BUSY, and the hum of conversation in the room disguises our silence throughout the meal. Even though I don't understand why, I wish I could take back the question about his brother. Not that I could have known it would trigger this kind of response, but because I can see how it has caused him pain. His clear blue eyes cannot hide it, and it feels as if the roots go deep.

To attempt small talk feels wrong. I want to say something that would help, but I have no idea what it might be.

His food is mostly untouched, and when the waitress brings our checks, he starts to sign them both to his room. I ask the waitress to put mine on my room because it feels weird not to. Ren looks at me and says, "I'm happy to get it."

"I know, but I want to," I say, suddenly aware that we are balancing in that strange place between friendship and attraction. I feel the awkwardness of it and have no idea what to do with it. I do not, however, want him to feel obligated to act as if it is anything other than what it is.

He concedes with a nod to the waitress, and once we've signed our checks, he looks at me and says, "I'm going to head out for a bit. Would you like for me to walk you back to your room?"

"No, I'm fine. You go."

"See you later," he says, pushing back his chair and walking from the room. As I watch him leave, I can almost feel the pent-up energy he's left behind. I wonder where he is going and if I should follow him. But that's crazy. Little more than a few days ago, we didn't even know each other. And it's a stretch to say we know each other now. Because we really don't. Nothing about the other that gets very far beneath the surface anyway.

I know all of this, and even so, I feel a little ragged edge of pain for whatever it is he's carrying around inside him.

I walk back to my room, the questions I most surely have no right to ask buzzing in my mind. I change into a pair of shorts and a tank top, hang my dress in the closet and sit down at the small desk.

I open my laptop with the intention of checking email. But my fingers go to the search engine icon instead. I type in: "Ren Sawyer brother death."

A flurry of articles pops up. I click on the first one. An article from the *LA Times*.

Rocker Killed in Bus Accident
Rock band Temporal lead guitarist Colby Sawyer was killed

last night in a single-vehicle accident while on tour in Oklahoma.

The Georgia-born band member sustained head injuries and died on arrival at Mercy Baptist Hospital. As lead guitarist for the band, Sawyer became a feature point in the group's concerts, finishing most shows with guitar solos that brought fans to their feet and kept them there until he disappeared from the stage.

Sawyer's brother, Ren Sawyer, lead singer for the band, could not be reached for comment.

I let the words sink in, feel the instant horror of them and at the same time, guilt for my online prying. If Ren had wanted me to know any of this, he would have told me earlier at the table.

Curiosity has become an itch that can be instantly scratched with search-engine access, and I guess I am no exception to the lure. I do not, however, let myself look further. I sit back. Based on his description of how he and his brother had started out together, I can only imagine how his death must have affected Ren.

I put on a pair of running shoes, shorts and shirt and leave the room without fully considering what I am doing. I take the stairs to the lobby and walk out into the courtyard. I wait there until I see him walking down the pea-gravel drive. Even from a distance, I can see that he is breathing heavily. When he gets closer, I also see that he is wet with sweat.

"Got anything left?" I ask.

He glances at my running shoes and says, "Yeah."

We head down the drive that leads around the back of the

hotel, follow a lighted path until it ends where a field begins. The moon is three-quarters full and casts enough light that we can see where our steps are taking us. The field goes on for a half-mile or so until it blends into an olive grove. We take a lane between two rows of trees and run on until we reach the end.

Our pace has been brisk, and I'm breathing hard. I bend over with my palms on my knees and reel in some air.

Ren's breathing has leveled out, and I wonder what his pace had been before he started running with me.

Once my breathing steadies a bit, I stand and look at the grove below us. The rows of trees are somewhat stacked so that we can see the tops below. The leaves are a silvery green under the moonlight, and I am filled with a sudden, swift love for this place. "It's so beautiful here," I say.

"It is," he agrees.

I drop to the ground, tuck my knees against my chest and push a hand through my damp hair. "Do you run a lot?" I ask.

"Not as much as I used to."

"I don't think you've lost your pace," I say.

"Just this little matter of not being able to breathe."

He gives me a half-smile but it feels more obligatory than amused. I pull a blade of grass from the ground and rub it between my forefinger and thumb.

"I'm sorry about all the questions at dinner," I say. "I didn't mean to be rude."

"You weren't," he says.

I prop an elbow on my knee, anchor my hand in my hair

and allow myself to fully look at him. He keeps his eyes averted from mine, and I take the opportunity to study his profile. It is an exceptionally beautiful one. His dark hair is longish and wavy, wet with sweat at the moment and raked back from his forehead.

His face is lean and chisel-cut. He obviously hasn't shaved in a couple of days. The stubble only adds to his appeal.

As if he feels me watching, he turns his head and our gazes clash head-on. The electric blue of his eyes sends a jolt of something so vibrant, so intense through me that I almost shiver with it.

We don't say anything; just study each other openly, with none of our previous censorship. "He's made you think you're not pretty, hasn't he?"

The question is so unexpected and so dead accurate that I blink beneath its insight. But I shrug, not acknowledging it either way.

"You are, you know," he says.

I wish I could say his words leave me neutral. But they don't. My cheeks warm under the compliment, and I glance away, unable to meet his eyes now. Even though it has not occurred to me until this exact moment, I realize exactly how much I want him to kiss me.

The thought is a completely new one because before now, it has not registered as a possibility. As strange and unlikely as it is that Ren and I would meet here and end up traveling around together, like college students on a spring break, it has been clear to me from the very beginning that even if

I weren't married, I'm not a woman who would ever fit into the life he leads or the women he dates. Before now, before this very moment when he is looking at me with raw desire on his face, I would have laughed at myself for even considering the possibility.

The inside of my chest seems to have suddenly caved in on itself, and I'm finding it hard to breathe normally. I feel myself tilt toward him as if I am being pulled forward by an invisible magnet, the force of which I have absolutely no power to resist. I should. I know it. I feel the *rat-a-tat-tat* of caution in my brain, and yet, it is a knock I have no inclination to answer.

Instead, something else swoops down on me, something wild and unlike anything I've ever felt in my life. I am not a rebel. I have never been one. I operate best within the rules. And here, the rules are clear. Married women don't kiss rock stars. But with that acknowledgment comes another. I don't feel married, haven't felt married for a very long time. And if I haven't felt married, I have felt even less desirable.

At some point in my marriage, I began to feel neutral. It didn't matter how long I searched for exactly the right dress, changed my makeup, switched my perfume, or added a few more highlights to my hair, it never really mattered because as soon as Ty looked at me, I felt sexless.

What else, after all, could you end up feeling? When no matter how hard you tried to be attractive to someone, if the end result was that they had no desire to touch you, to make love to you, clearly whatever you once had that attracted him was gone. Dried up like grapes left in the sun for days on end and in no way resembling what they had once been.

But here under this man's lust-filled surmisal–and yes, I did say lust–I am transformed. Dried up is not a phrase that in any way applies to how I currently feel. It is as if my entire being has been turned to liquid. Warm ocean waves lapping up from a yearning place that has not yearned in what seems like forever.

When he leans in and kisses me, I am completely submerged beneath those waves. I want to drown in them. The kiss is anything but tentative. No questioning. A simple and declarative taking. I want nothing more than to give. I meet his intensity with a response I would never have imagined as coming from me.

I am a well, capped off as no longer needed. But the springs that feed it have a continuous need for release. I did not know my own need. Am only now recognizing the force behind it.

We kiss for what feels like both a minute and forever all at the same time. I don't want him to stop. I never imagined that kissing could be like this, an all-out mockery of anything I have experienced. Like believing fire never burned beyond lukewarm, only to touch the flame and realize the extent to which it can blaze red-hot.

Our ragged breathing stands out from the night sounds in the grove. On some level, I know we should stop. But stronger than that is the fact that I don't want to.

For my entire adult life, I have done as I should, whether

by guilt or obligation, when choice was in question. But this time, I will not be the one to cave.

Ren pulls me to him, physically lifting me so that I am now straddling his lap, a knee on either side of his hips. His hands slip under my T-shirt and splay my waist. All the while, he never stops kissing me, deep, artful kissing that makes me wonder how it is possible that I have reached the age of thirty-eight and never once felt this way.

I loop my arms around his neck and press into him, wanting to touch every accessible part of him. His hands are now anchored in my hair, and I can feel the certainty of how quickly we are going to another place. He again lifts me and puts me on my back, stretches out on top of me, his long, hard legs pressing into mine.

I feel the damp earth beneath my back and yield to it as he yields to me.

But when he rolls off me a moment later to lie staring up at the night sky, his chest rising and falling with the effort of breathing, I feel as if something now vital has been torn from me.

I have only been aware of its existence for mere minutes, but it is now critical to my own existence, like my heart that pumps the blood throughout my body, my lungs that pull in necessary oxygen.

Neither of us speaks for a minute or more. His voice is thick with something I'm hesitant to identify when he says, "I'm not a good guy, Lizzy."

It's pretty much the last thing I would have expected him

to say. I'm not at all sure how to take it. I turn my head to look at him and wonder if he is simply trying to find an out. "Ren. You don't have to feel guilty about this. Or make excuses. You're not taking advantage of me, if that's what you're thinking."

He makes a sound that is half laugh, half "hah." "I wish I were guilty of something as simple as that, Lizzy."

I have a sudden, overwhelming urge to cry. I don't know how it is possible to go through the gamut of emotions I've experienced since we left the hotel in Florence. It feels as if I've just learned how to fly. High above the treetops like the bald eagle I once saw as a little girl. And just when I have begun to appreciate how incredible the view is from way up there, my wings become weighted with something I don't understand, and I am hurled back to the ground.

"I haven't seen anything," I say, "that would make me believe that could be true."

"It is," he says. "Believe me."

I hear the adamant conviction beneath the words and wonder what he is hanging his self-condemnation on. "Ren," I start.

But he stands, holds out a hand and pulls me up in front of him. I tip forward, and my palm automatically goes to his chest to right myself. I hear his sharp intake of breath, and I can't deny that I feel some satisfaction in knowing that maybe it isn't any easier for him to pull away from me than it is for me to let him.

We stand very still, studying each other, trapped beneath

the moonlight. I want him to change his mind, go back to where we were, finish what we started.

I should be ashamed to admit it. I should be. But I'm not.

He laces his fingers through mine, and we walk back to the hotel that way, hand in hand. And I have the distinct feeling that he is forcing himself to turn away from me. That maybe he doesn't really want to. That if we were different people with different lives, this might go somewhere beyond fulfillment of the immediate. And as we cross the field, back into the lights flowing out from the hotel, I think that maybe just knowing that should be enough to fill the emptiness inside of me.

22

Ren

SLEEP IS PRETTY MUCH a wasted effort. I lie awake, staring at the ceiling and trying to talk myself into agreeing with what I already know. I should pack my stuff and leave first thing in the morning. Before Lizzy is even awake.

That would be the kindest thing, for both of us.

It takes me a couple of hours, but by five a.m., this is what I've talked myself into.

I get out of bed, stand under the shower for a good fifteen minutes, letting the cool spray wash away enough fatigue that I can think about facing the day without sleep.

Once I'm dressed, I pull a piece of hotel stationery from a desk drawer, find a pen and sit down to write her a note.

It's a chicken-shit thing to do in light of what almost happened between us last night. Even I can admit that. She deserves far better, and I'm not it.

Lizzy,
I'm not what you need. I'd like to be, but I'm not. I hope that
whoever is, deserves you.
Ren

I fold the paper and put it in an envelope, seal it shut and write her name on the front. I throw what few things I have into my bag and leave the room.

I take the stairs to the lobby and before I get to the front desk, I hear a man speaking in a very loud voice to the clerk. I stop just short, pull my wallet from my jacket so that I can clear out the bill. He's obviously upset about something, and then I hear him say her name.

"Elizabeth Harper."

He says it slowly and concisely, as if the woman standing in front of him is deaf.

"*Signore* Harper. It is not our policy to reveal the guests staying at our hotel. Do you have a number you could use to call her? A cell phone perhaps?"

I realize then who must be standing in front of me.

Her husband.

Ty, I believe she said his name was.

He's built like a football player, broad-shouldered, five-tenish. His hair is sandy blonde and military short. He has an air about him that suggests he's used to getting his requests met, and quickly. Means business. No nonsense.

"If you do not give me her room number immediately, I will go door to door and knock until I find the correct one. I know she's here. Her credit card was used last night at this restaurant."

The woman studies him for a moment, her expression one of clear disapproval, but I can see her yielding as if she believes he will do what he has just threatened.

"Let me see what I can do, Signore Harper. I will call to the manager."

"You do that," he says, his tone clipped.

As if sensing that I'm here, he turns and looks at me. I stare back at him, and I can see instantly that it makes him uncomfortable, as if he isn't used to being called down for bad behavior.

He glances away, shifts from one foot to the other and then clears his throat. "I have ID to prove who I am, and they still won't tell me which room my wife is in."

"Hm," I say, nodding. "Bummer."

The clerk has disappeared through a door behind the front desk. I drop my bag to the floor, fold my arms across my chest. He looks back at me again, studies me for a moment, as if he thinks he should know who I am. I see the recognition dawn on his face.

"Hey. Aren't you Ren . . . Sawyer?"

"Yeah. I am."

He brightens and becomes instantly amicable. "My daughter likes your music, man. I like your music."

"Thanks," I say.

"Sorry to look like such an ass, but I've been trying to track my wife down for a few days now."

"Is she lost?" I ask, straight-faced.

His eyes squint a little as if he's not sure how to take my question. "No. We . . . it's just kind of a misunderstanding, I guess."

"Really? What kind of misunderstanding?"

He rakes a hand through his short hair, beginning to look as if he's sorry he started this conversation.

"*Signore* Harper." The front desk clerk walks back out, forces a smile and says, "I have spoken with our manager, and—"

I raise a hand behind Harper's back and wave slightly to get her attention. She glances at me, and I shake my head in a small gesture. I see her blink, look from me to Harper and back again.

"And our manager has said that is not possible at this time. If she is indeed staying here, we will contact her at an hour when it is acceptable to phone. We will inform her that you are here, if that is the case."

If fury in another person can be felt, Antonia and I are definitely feeling Harper's.

"Is there a place where I can get some coffee while I wait?" he asks, the words pinched and tight.

"Yes, in our café. It will be open in just a few minutes. Please, go in and make yourself comfortable."

He drops her a curt nod, and then, glancing back at me, says, "Nice talking with you."

"You too," I say, and watch him walk away.

Once he is out of sight, I hand Antonia my credit card and say, "Could you please clear out both my room and Mrs. Harper's bill?"

"Signora Harper is quite popular today," she says, a small smile on her mouth.

"Thanks for that," I say. "I appreciate it."

"Of course, Mr. Sawyer," she says. "And I like your music too."

"Thank you," I say, and for once in recent history, I'm actually glad she knows who I am if it helped prevent Harper from going upstairs.

"You are welcome."

I grab my bag, the letter I had just written to Lizzy still in my hand. I think of how easily her husband could have noticed it. I wonder if I should leave as planned. Give her a chance to make things up with him. Even as I climb the stairs to her room, I'm not sure why I'm doing this. For her? So that she can make her own decision about whether to see him or not. Or for me? Because I don't want to leave her, after all.

I tap on her door with the back of my knuckles, lightly. I hear her call out, "Yes?"

"Lizzy, it's me."

"Ren?" She opens the door and sticks her head around, sleepy-eyed. "What is it? Are you all right?"

"Yeah. I just saw your husband downstairs."

She is suddenly as wide-awake as if I had doused her with ice water. "What? How do you know?"

"I heard him trying to get Antonia at the front desk to tell him which room you're in."

"It's barely five-thirty. What were you doing at the front desk?"

"We might want to get out of here," I say, avoiding her question.

"But—"

"I paid for our rooms. Do you want to go or stay?" I see the confusion on her face, but it only takes a couple of seconds for it to be replaced with resolution.

"Give me three minutes," she says.

I stand outside the door in the hallway, wondering exactly what I'm going to say if he shows up before we manage to get out of here. But Lizzy is right on the mark, and three minutes later, we're taking the back stairs to the parking lot.

I open the door and follow her through. We run, our bags jostling on our shoulders, to the Fiat. She hits the remote lock. We throw our luggage in the back and jump in. I get in on the passenger side, not quite as easily. She starts the car and guns it out of the parking lot, spitting pea gravel down the long drive to the main road.

We drive for ten minutes with neither of us saying anything. She's gripping the steering wheel so hard that the backs of her fingers are nearly white.

"You're fine," I say.

"A vigilante," she says, irony underlining the word. "On the run."

"As soon as you want to be caught, you can stop running," I say.

She looks at me, and I again see the question in her eyes, even before she voices it. "Why were you downstairs so early with your bag packed?"

I can't bring myself to be anything but honest with her. "I thought it would be best if I left," I say. I expect her to disagree, but she doesn't.

"It probably would have been. Why didn't you?"

"I'm not really sure," I say. "Was I wrong to let you know he was there?"

She shakes her head. "Thank you."

"I'd like to say I just did it for you, but I'm not sure that would be the truth."

She looks at me then. Something softens in her eyes. She quickly blinks it away, as if recognizing her vulnerability. She puts her gaze back on the road. "I kind of wanted to see San Gimignano."

"San Gimignano, it is," I say.

23

Ty

YOU SIT IN THE small cafe off the main lobby of the hotel, sipping a far-too-strong-for-your-taste coffee while you practice every speck of temper control you can summon up.

A ten-hour flight across the Atlantic, in coach because there were no last-minute seats available in first class. That miserable experience, and then you finally arrive here only to find that Lizzy has checked out of the hotel in Florence. That she isn't even in the city. Having to track her down by your credit-card statement.

Your shirt collar suddenly feels tight around your neck. You run a finger around the rim and blow out a breath of disbelief. The Lizzy you're married to would never do something like this. Then again, she's never been told before that you are cheating on her. Or at least you don't think so.

A waitress in a white uniform comes to the table every fifteen minutes or so and asks if she can get you anything else. You notice that she never quite meets your eyes, and you start to wonder if you've missed something.

What kind of hotel refuses to give a husband the room number of his wife? Of course they would be taking your word for it, but you do have ID, and you do have the same last name.

You drum your fingers on the tabletop, replaying the scene at the front desk when the clerk had said you would have to wait until a more reasonable hour. You had been sure she was about to say something entirely different. But then she had glanced at Sawyer. You still can't believe he was standing right behind you.

Had something passed between the two of them, or was your imagination simply working overtime? And what could it possibly have to do with Lizzy and your wanting to see her?

You have no idea, but something doesn't feel right. As an attorney, you long ago learned to trust your gut. To listen to it, even in the face of evidence to the contrary.

And your gut is telling you that Sawyer had signaled the clerk not to give him the information.

The question is, why?

24

Kylie

IT'S THREE O'CLOCK in the morning, and Kylie wants to go back to her dorm.

Now that some of her alcoholic haze has started to recede, she raises up on one arm to squint at her surroundings. The hotel room is just this side of repulsive. There's a smell that makes her stomach twitch.

She glances at Jack, stretched out beside her on the paper-thin white sheets and wonders if she should wake him to walk her back.

The almost empty bottle of rum on the nightstand catches her eye, and she recalls exactly how intoxicated he had been just before passing out in the middle of kissing her. That's where the fantasy had come to a startling stop. Rock star in the making. Out of all the girls at the club that night, he had picked her.

Only now did she think regrettably.

She swings her legs over the side of the bed, stands and teeters slightly, grabbing onto the bed's headboard to steady herself. She finds her clothes piece by piece, realizing what a waste it had been to take them off.

Once she's dressed, she goes into the bathroom, turns on the faucet and uses her hand to scoop water into her mouth. It tastes like the room smells. She spits it out and longs for some mouthwash.

She gropes around the darkened room until she finds her purse and phone, considers calling a cab, but then decides it would take too long to wait. She just wants to get back to her room and into her own bed, with its clean sheets and fat pillow. The dorm is only a mile or so from where she is, and since she can run that in under seven minutes, walking shouldn't take so much longer, even in the shoes she's wearing.

She lets herself out of the room without looking back at Jack, reluctant to further tarnish what little remains of her earlier hopes for the night.

The motel parking lot is dimly lit, at best, and she sets off down the street that leads back to campus with purpose in her stride, her phone clutched in her right hand. She hears a dog barking somewhere in the distance, traffic sounds from the nearby highway. She can feel her heart thumping with her pace, anxiety accelerating its beat more than the exertion.

Five minutes into the walk, she's starting to think this might have been a mistake. There's absolutely no one around. It's as if the whole town has disappeared. She can still call a taxi, but the thought of stopping and waiting makes her quicken her stride. The dorm can't be more than ten minutes away, at the most.

She focuses on her pace, counting the steps in an effort to tamp back her fear. It works because she can no longer feel her heart pounding against the wall of her chest. The dorm building appears in the distance, and she starts to sweat with relief. She thinks of all the times her mom has told her not to do things like this. "Don't ever put yourself in a position of vulnerability, Kylie. Bad people look for opportunity."

She hears the words as if her mother is standing beside her. She knows that is exactly what she has just done, and she feels a slight flare of gladness that her mother hasn't been proved right, this time anyway.

With the building in sight, she slows her pace a bit, her breathing less of an effort.

She glances at her phone, checking for text messages. There's one from Peyton.

Where are you?

She's just started to tap in an answer when she hears the car behind her. The engine is loud, and it's as if the sound has dropped from the sky. She turns to look at it, the headlights blinding her for a moment. She raises a hand to block the glare, but it doesn't help.

The car screeches to a stop beside her, the passenger side door opening. Fear grabs her by the throat, and she bolts, knowing in that instant that she should run.

She focuses on the sounds of her own footsteps, pounding

on the concrete sidewalk. She can't tell if anyone is behind her. It's only when she feels the hand grab her arm and jerk her to a halt that the scream breaks free from her throat.

Her phone slides from her grip and skitters away just before she lands with a thud on the unforgiving surface of the sidewalk. A grunt of pain erupts from her throat, but even as it does, she's fighting to get up.

He's too strong though, too big. Her efforts are puny, pathetic.

The car roars up beside them. The man picks her up as if she is a ball of fluff, opens the back door and shoves her inside. Her left shoulder hits the other side of the car, and pain flashes red in front of her eyes.

He gets in the back seat with her, slams the door. The car peels away from the curb, shooting off into the night just as consciousness recedes from her vision, and the night is no more.

25

Ren

WE DRIVE FOR forty-five minutes before Lizzy mentions stopping for coffee. I'm dying for a cup, but I figured she would rather put some distance between us and the likelihood of Harper catching up.

A small sign on the side of the road says **Ristorante** with an arrow pointing right and then it reads, **2 Km.**

Lizzy points at it and says, "Sound good?"

"Yeah."

She swings the Fiat into the turn. We blow dust up the dirt road that winds past one clay-tile roof house after another until a second sign declaring **Ristorante** appears, and we turn into the parking lot.

The outside is plain enough. White stucco. Tile roof.

Shutters that droop a little at the edges. Window box flowers add some color.

Inside, we are greeted with the smells of bread baking in an oven and roasting coffee beans.

A round-faced woman who introduces herself as the proprietor leads us to a table and asks us what we would like. In my rag-tag Italian, I manage to convey two Caffé Americanos and bread.

She nods in approval, disappears to the kitchen and returns moments later with a French press pot of coffee and two cups. She pours for us both, sets a pitcher of cream and a dish of sugar cubes on the table, then heads back to the kitchen.

Lizzy and I sip in silent appreciation.

"So good," she says.

I nod, and then say, "He and I talked a bit."

Her gaze pops up to mine.

"Your . . . Ty." I start to say husband but somehow can't bring myself to say the word.

"I . . . what did you say?"

"Small talk. Said he liked my music."

Her eyes go wide then. "He recognized you."

I shrug.

"Did he know that you and I—"

I shake my head. "I managed to convey to Antonia, the front-desk clerk, that she shouldn't tell him where you were. He seemed pretty frazzled."

She takes another sip of her coffee. "He's not used to being bested."

"Has he been?"

"For the moment, anyway."

"Did you know he was coming?"

She glances away and then back at me. "He sent a fax to the hotel in Florence that he would be arriving late yesterday morning."

"Ah. Hence the hasty departure."

"Yeah," she says.

The proprietor brings us a basket of fresh-out-of-the-oven pastries and two glasses of orange juice. We eat in silence for a few minutes. And then, because it has begun to feel like the elephant in the middle of the room, I force myself to say, "Lizzy. What happened last night—"

"Don't," she says quickly, an expression closely resembling pain crossing her face. "Really. Let's not go there, okay?"

"I just want you to know that—"

"There's nothing to know that I don't already know. Nothing about any of this has made a grain of sense. Least of all that."

I want to tell her that she is wrong, that nothing has made as much sense to me in longer than I can remember. But I know that to do so would be to act as if what I said last night wasn't true.

Only, it is true.

We finish our coffee in silence. I pick up the check and pay at the front register, ignoring Lizzy's protest that she will pay for her own.

In the parking lot, a man in a white cook's apron is yelling something in Italian and chasing a small, very dirty, very matted, possibly once white puppy around a large cypress tree.

The puppy can't be more than a few months old and is carrying, more like dragging, what looks like a large soup bone in its small mouth. The man's face is red, his voice rising with another sputter of angry Italian. He claps his hands together hard. The puppy drops the bone and runs straight under the Fiat.

I can tell by the look on Lizzy's face that none of this has settled well with her. The round woman comes out of the restaurant then, spouting off something to the man in equally angry Italian. She points to the door and makes a shooing motion for him to go back inside. She looks at us and shakes her head. "No patience, that one. Someone has left the dog here, a few days ago. I have been feeding a bit, but if I keep doing so, it will not leave."

"Maybe it could stay?" Lizzy suggests.

She shakes her head. "It is covered with the fleas. Not good for *ristorante* patrons."

Lizzy drops down on her knees beside the car, peers under one door and makes a patting motion for the puppy to come out. From the other side of the car, I drop down and look under to see that it is huddled in a small, dirty ball, shaking like the only leaf left on an end of fall oak tree.

I sit back while Lizzy coaxes and sweet talks. But the puppy isn't budging, so I decide to give it a try. I walk around to the driver's side, stretch flat out on the ground with my head on my forearms and start talking to him.

It is still shaking so hard that I think I actually hear the poor thing's teeth chattering.

Footsteps sound on the gravel drive. The round woman is back, assuring us that we will be able to leave momentarily since she has called the animal *polizia*. They are on their way.

I look at Lizzy and see the instantly stricken look on her face. I have to admit I feel a plummet of fear for the little guy myself.

"What will they do?" Lizzy asks.

"They have pole thing with hook to pull him out."

Lizzy looks at me with a near-frantic expression.

"I will be inside if you need me," the woman says.

"We can't let them take him," Lizzy cries, as soon as she leaves. "Maybe I can crawl under there."

"He's scared," I say. "He might bite you. He's young, but still—"

"What else can we do?"

I turn over on my back, stare up at the sky and do the only thing I know how to do. I start to sing, a low hum at first and then find the words to a song I wrote with Colby when we were just kids.

First chance to win this fight
Last chance to get it right
Come on now, you know it's true
Give up now, and it's all through

Make up your mind
Can't take your time

"His ears are perked," Lizzy whispers. "Keep going."

And so I do. Snatches of one song or another for ten minutes before he starts to crawl toward me on his belly until Lizzy says, "It's working."

I feel my heart beating really fast and realize how much I want him to come to me. I'm still humming softly when I feel his small chin drop onto my shoulder. I reach my hand back to scratch his side, feel the mats in his fur and wonder how anyone could leave something so young and vulnerable to fend for itself.

I hear the crunch of gravel on the drive.

"It's them!" Lizzy says, jumping to her feet.

I reach my other hand back, scoop the puppy up and stand. Lizzy gets in the driver's side. I walk around with the pup tucked out of sight and get in the other door. She starts the Fiat and eases out of the lot, waving at the truck as we roll by.

"Just in the nick of time," I say, looking at Lizzy.

She smiles a really beautiful smile, her eyes softening with something real and true.

"Who says you're not a good guy?" she asks.

26

Ty

YOU COME AWAKE to the realization that you fell asleep at some point, despite the strong coffee.

Morning sounds echo around you, the clink of dishes from the nearby kitchen, conversations taking place at nearby tables.

You sit up and rake a hand through your hair, glancing at your watch. How could you have slept this long? You get to your feet, feeling the leaden weight of jet lag. Leaving your bags where they are, you walk quickly across the lobby to the front desk.

A young man is now behind the counter. He looks up at you and smiles. "*Buon giorno, signore.* How might I help you?"

You don't return his ridiculously white smile. "My wife is staying in the hotel. Can you call her room and let her know I'm here?"

"Certainly, s*ignore*. What is her name?"

"Lizzy Harper."

"One moment." He checks the computer, taps a few keys, and then says, "Ah, I am sorry, s*ignore*. But it appears that your wife has already checked out."

27

Lizzy

"WHAT EXACTLY DO we do now that we've saved him?" I ask, maneuvering the Fiat through another small town.

"Good question," Ren says.

As it turns out, he is a she, which Ren soon discovers after holding her up for inspection.

"Think we ought to find a vet or something?" I ask.

"It kind of looks like she could use one," he says.

The puppy is now curled up on his lap, sound asleep as if she hasn't slept in days. Which considering her current state of survival, she probably hasn't. "Can you Google one?" I ask.

"If I can figure out how to type in veterinarian in Italian," he says.

"Use the translator – English to Italian."

"Do you think Google has already thought of everything, or is there more to come?" Ren asks.

"I suspect there's more to come," I say.

Ren spends a couple of minutes tapping and typing and finally says, "Here's one. It's ten miles away. Should we go for it?"

"Yep," I say. "Is your GPS going to tell me where to go?"

"It most certainly is," he says with a smile.

"You have to give her a name," I say, tipping my head toward the puppy.

"Kind of hard to tell what she looks like under all the dirt."

"We should assume the best. Something to live up to. How about Sophia? As in the actress. Italian, too."

He considers it, and then says, "Sophia. Definitely a name to grow into. Sophia, it is."

Ren's GPS is a little off on its calculations, so we spend ten minutes or so weaving through the cobblestone streets until we find a green door with a medical sign hanging above, a picture of a dog beside it.

I squeeze the car into a miniscule parking place. Sophia is back to shaking, her head tucked under Ren's arm.

"Don't worry, little bean," he says. "We're just getting you checked out."

But she's not buying it and tries to burrow herself between the buttonholes of his shirt. "I might end up with the fleas," Ren says, smiling.

A very pretty Italian veterinary assistant greets us at the front desk. Fortunately for us, she speaks some English. Ren manages to explain how we found the puppy and would like to have her checked out and given any necessary shots. She nods in understanding, starting a file. She asks his name, and, to my surprise, he tells her his real name. She doesn't appear to recognize it though and asks for the puppy's name.

"Sophia," he says. "Would it be possible to give her a bath and take care of these mats in her coat? They have to be making her miserable."

"Of course, *signore*. Can you leave her for two hours?"

We agree that will be fine. She picks up Sophia who looks at Ren with completely mournful eyes as if she is sure she will never see him again. I can see in his face that he's struck by her sadness.

"We'll be back, little girl," he says. "Don't worry." But as we're walking out the clinic door, he looks at me and adds, "She doesn't believe that, does she?"

"Probably not," I say.

We stroll through the town, find some amazing views and sit in a small park watching some older men play a game I've never seen before. I glance at Ren. "What are they doing?"

"It's called b*occie*. Goes back to ancient Rome."

"They look serious about it."

Ren nods. "Pretty good life, isn't it?"

The men are laughing, clearly enjoying themselves, despite how intent they are about winning. "It looks that way," I say.

"Do you ever think maybe we should live more of our lives like that?" he asks.

"Like what?"

"Just hanging out, not always chasing after something."

"I don't know. When we're younger, we feel like we have something to prove. Sometimes, to ourselves. Sometimes, to others. Maybe when we've done that, we start looking for some other kind of fulfillment. Is that where you are?" I ask.

He lifts his shoulders in a shrug that seems to say he really doesn't know. "Most people would call me crazy for saying so. Maybe I am crazy."

"You're you. And you're entitled to be who you want to be."

"I don't think I know the answer to that anymore," he says.

I hear something in his voice that I haven't heard before. Raw honesty. Revealing and questioning. "What is it that you don't want anymore?"

He doesn't answer for so long that I think he's not going to. That maybe I've been way too forward in asking the questions. "Being me," he finally says.

I hear the layers in the answer. Something tells me that it is directly tied to the statement he made last night. *I'm not a good guy.*

We leave the park and grab a slice of pizza from a little place across the street.

As proof of Ren's concern about Sophia, we arrive back at the veterinary office exactly two hours from the time we left her there. The same girl is at the front. She greets us with a smile and says, "Ah, Sophia. You will not recognize her."

"Is she in good health?" Ren asks.

"I let doctor explain," she says. "Please to come this way."

She leads us into a small room where we wait for a couple of minutes until the door opens again and a white-haired man with spectacles that sit on the tip of his nose steps inside and greets us with a polite nod. "*Signore. Signora?*"

"Hello," we answer in unison.

"I'm Dr. Giardino. Your Sophia is fourteen to sixteen weeks old." He opens the file that now has her name on it.

"You found her?"

"Yes. This morning," Ren replies.

"Lucky for her, yes?" the doctor says with a smile. "She has many fleas. We have treated for this. And also for parasites. I have given her medicine for this, and we will also be sending some along with you."

The door opens again, and the girl from the front comes in, holding Sophia. "Oh, my goodness, you're beautiful," I say.

She brightens at my voice and then looks at Ren, her tail starting to wag instantly.

"You did live up to your name, Sophia," he says, reaching out to take her from the girl.

The puppy is all wiggles and waggles, licking his face, clearly overjoyed that he has returned, after all. Ren melts under her lavishing of attention, laughs and then tucks her up under his arm where she still manages to wiggle her butt in glee and joy.

The doctor laughs. "She was very shy with us, but with you, no."

"Thank you," Ren says, "for taking care of her and so quickly."

"You are most welcome," he says. "If there is anything else we can do for you, please ask." He opens the door and leads us back out front where a young woman now prints the bill. Ren takes it and then hands her a credit card.

She runs it through the machine, gives him a paper to sign and says, "Thank you for coming."

We turn to leave just as Dr. Giardino says, "*Signore* Sawyer?"

Ren turns back and the older man looks a bit embarrassed.

"Would you very much mind signing something for Annetta here and the other three ladies in the back? They are beside themselves that you have visited us today."

"Actually, I'd be really honored to do that," Ren says.

As if they have been listening at the door, three young women file into the lobby. One, sixteen at the most, the other two in their twenties. They stand slightly behind Dr. Giardino, unable to actually look at Ren.

"Hello," he says to them with the smile I am certain has won him thousands of fans just like them. "Thank you so much for taking care of Sophia."

They raise their eyes and smile at him, shy and charming in their appeal. Dr. Giardino moves over to stand beside them, and they each hold out an item for Ren to sign. A long sleeve T-shirt with the clinic logo, a note card and two of his CDs. They are overcome with giggles, and I find myself smiling at their astonishment that they have found themselves in this position today.

When he's finished signing, one of the girls reaches out to give her a rub. "Lucky Sophia," she says.

They thank him again profusely.

We walk out the door accompanied by many well wishes. Once we are out on the street, I rub Sophia's soft, now silky, coat and say, "Who knew you were such a beauty?"

She wags her tail and licks my hand. I am happy to see I'm also working my way into her good graces.

We get in the car, and as I maneuver through the small town streets, Ren tells his GPS to take us to San Gimignano. We have not exited the town limits before Sophia is again asleep on his lap, curled up in a small poufy ball.

"You saved her," I say.

"So did you," he says.

"I think it was you she was waiting for. You're the one who was meant to find her."

I say it lightly, but I really do mean it.

He rubs the puppy's back and looks out the window. "I guess we all need saving some time or other, don't we?"

There's a note in his voice I haven't heard before. I can't actually put a name to it. I just know it puts a clamp on my heart and squeezes so tight that it hurts.

28

Kylie

SHE CAN HEAR voices. Men's voices.

At first, it sounds as if there are a dozen or more, words strung together in bits and pieces. She struggles to recognize their meaning, but can absorb nothing. They ping from the surface of comprehension like hail off a tin roof.

She tries to open her eyes. They're so heavy. It's as if they've been wired shut. Or stapled. She feels a tear seep through, slide down her cheek.

Her body hurts. Everywhere. She tries to force her brain to command movement. From her legs. Her arms. There's no response. She's trapped under a lead net, flattened by it, a moth in a spider web.

A word breaks through. A word she understands. *Money.* What follows she cannot make out. The voice rises with anger. *If damaged. No money.* Those four words crack like lightning in the distance.

What are they talking about? If what is damaged?

They want them untouched. Clean. Do you understand that?

I understand. Do I agree? No.

No one cares if you agree. Touch her, and you get nothing! Do you understand that?

Silence echoes around the question.

Kylie tries to scream. Tries to force her eyes open. But the lead net is still in place. And the only response she can summon her body to make is the single tear she feels sliding down her cheek.

29

Ren

SOPHIA AND I sit under a covered arch and watch while Lizzy shoots photo after photo, moving from one spot to another, quickly and efficiently, snapping, snapping, like a child in a candy store who can't grab fast enough.

On the way here, she told me about the popularity of San Gimignano with photographers and how the light at sunset was supposed to be amazing.

It's just after four-thirty now, and the light is every bit as beautiful as Lizzy had predicted. It's hard to explain, really, without seeing it for yourself. But it's special, and even though I'm no photographer, I can see it.

Sophia is again snoozing on my knee. I rub under her chin in a methodical rhythm that elicits from her a near purring sound. I wonder how long it will take her to finally feel rested.

Lizzy stands at the top of an angled set of stairs, shooting down into the square, and then, tipping her camera upward, aimed at an angle of roof and sky. Her love for what she is doing is so obvious that I feel a pang of sadness to think she spent so many years without it. I can only equate it with my music and how much a part of me it has always been. Leaving it alone would be like getting up in the morning and trying not to breathe in air.

She's wearing jeans, the skinny kind, and a white tank top that scoops low in the front. Her arms are long and finely muscled the way lifelong runners tend to be. Her thick blonde hair is pulled back in a loose ponytail, the band midway down between her shoulders so that wisps of it escape around her face and cling to her cheeks.

My gaze falls across her mouth, her lips full and soft as I now know them to be. And suddenly, I'm thinking about last night and the unexpectedness of wanting her in a way I've never wanted anyone before.

On the surface, I'll be the first to admit that it makes little to no sense. Aside from this time together here, our lives are about as different as it is possible for two lives to be. I don't understand it, and yet I can't deny how it feels to be with her. How the weight that has sat on my chest for the past three years is no longer so heavy that I don't think I can ever push myself out from under it. It's still there, but something is starting to occur to me.

I don't want the weight to be there anymore. And that hasn't been true since the day Colby died.

I've welcomed the boulder of guilt that crushed from me even the desire to go on living. Why now? Why this woman? I came here at peace with the realization that life as I have been leading it, is a life I no longer want to live.

And even beyond that, deserve to live.

That piece of my decision has never changed. Will never change. I know I'm not the one who should be here, continuing on with what Colby and I had built together. He's the one who should be here.

Even if Lizzy has opened a door in me, let in a slip of light, of hope, none of that erases this second truth.

She drops her camera to her chest, lifts a hand and waves at us. Her smile hooks something low inside me and literally brings me to my feet, walking me across the square to where she is standing.

"You have to see," she says, flipping the back of the camera open and clicking through some of the images she's just taken. "It's incredible. More than I ever imagined."

"They're beautiful, Lizzy. The setting is beautiful. But so is your interpretation."

She looks up at me then, and I nearly regret the words. I see how they validate her, and I wish that it were someone else bringing this feeling alive in her. Someone who is not me.

She reaches out then and presses her palm to my face. Her touch is like electricity surging through me, turning off my brain to all reason. I dip in and kiss her, fully, without any attempt to hide exactly how much I want to kiss her.

Her camera is pressed between the two of us. She places her

other hand on it and then slides her fingers up my chest until they are at the side of my face, her touch tender in a way that breaks something inside me. I change the tone of the kiss to reflect that same tenderness.

Sophia wiggles under my arm, but I'm unwilling to end this kiss any sooner than I have to. A low sound of want breaks free from Lizzy's throat. She pulls back, touches a finger to her lower lip and then drops her head onto my chest. We say nothing. It seems pointless. Right or wrong, this thing between us is something I have no desire to continue resisting. Even if I know how wrong I am not to.

"Will you let me decide what kind of guy you are?" she asks, her voice low and soft.

"Lizzy."

But she pulls my face to hers and kisses me in a way that tells me she's already made up her mind. I only wish I could live up to her conclusion.

30

Lizzy

WE FIND A SMALL hotel near the walled entrance of the town. It's charming and rustic. The man at the front desk is as happy to see Sophia as he is to see us. He leads us up the stairs to the third floor where our rooms are side by side.

He's carrying a pillow for Sophia and two bowls that he pilfered from the downstairs kitchen, one for water and one that he's filled with some chunks of chicken the cook allowed him to take for the puppy.

Our rooms do not have an adjoining door, and by now, I am telling myself this is a good thing. We agree to meet downstairs in an hour or so. I take a shower, blow dry my hair and plug my camera into my laptop. I upload the pictures from this afternoon. They're even better than I had hoped they would be.

I cull the ones with obvious flaws, and then choose those I absolutely love, putting them into a separate file.

All of the photos focus on some facet of the square, an architectural element, the skyline above. Except for one. This one, I took of Ren when he was sitting under a covered arch with Sophia. He hadn't been aware of my lens, and his face is without concealment. He is looking at Sophia with already bonded affection.

I find it hard to sync the man I see in front of me with the one Ren is so certain exists. Does he? And if so, why have I not seen him? People are only so good at concealing their true nature. Or at least that is what I once thought. Using Ty as an example, I guess I would be dead wrong.

I actually haven't let myself think about Ty even once in the past several hours. I'm not sure that it's been deliberate. Maybe on some level, but on another, I feel like someone completely different with Ren.

And I am different. Have I ever known this version of me? Someone who can live in the moment? Not try to predict what will happen at the end of this trip? At the end of this week? This day?

I don't think so.

For dinner, I put on a flowy skirt in a shade of magenta that I've always loved, but mostly felt was too bold for any of the things I attended at home. I add a white tank top and flat sandals, lipstick in the same shade of magenta.

I'm downstairs before Ren, and I wait by the front door, feeling nervous for reasons I can't exactly pinpoint.

I hear him on the stairs before I see him. Butterflies assault my midsection. He's wearing jeans and a white shirt. His dark hair is still wet from the shower. I feel an undeniable urge to run my fingers through it.

He meets my gaze with a smile. It's not a bold, confident smile, but has something uncertain at its edges. I'm caught off guard by it. Uncertainty is the last thing I would expect from him.

"Is Sophia out for the count?" I ask, inexplicably nervous.

"Yeah, she's nearly in a coma."

I smile. "We'll have to bring her a snack."

He nods, opens the door, and we step out into the cool night. The cobblestones are uneven beneath our feet.

"So where to?" he asks.

"Want to just walk until something looks good?"

"Sure," he says.

We turn right, heading up the incline of the street.

"It's called the town of fine towers," I say, glancing up at the tall structures that once represented the wealthy families who lived here. "It's unsettling to think that thousands of years ago, people walked these same streets."

"I read that the Black Death killed about two-thirds of the citizens in 1300 or so," Ren says. "They went from thirteen thousand citizens to four thousand in something like six months."

"How horrible," I say.

"The town mostly stays the same," he says. "We're the ones who come and go."

We walk in silence for the next few minutes, checking out menus of little places we pass until one in particular resonates with us both. It's small and rustic, and Ren has to duck a bit going through the door. Copper pots hang from beamed ceilings. Farm tables with wood chairs provide the seating in the room.

We're greeted by a young Italian man in a dark suit, the formality contrasting with the more casual décor of the place. He leads us to a table in the middle of the restaurant. Several other tables are already occupied by diners intent on conversation and eating.

We sit and study our menus in silence for a couple of minutes until it becomes awkward.

"Will he follow you here?"

I look up, a little startled by the question. It's the first time Ren has spoken since we sat down at the table. "I honestly don't know," I say.

"He seems like a persistent guy," Ren says.

I can't deny this. Winning is as much a part of Ty's genetic makeup as the DNA that contributed to his blonde hair and green eyes. I suspect that my leaving Florence the way I had was pretty much the same thing as throwing down a gauntlet of challenge as far as Ty is concerned. "If he does," I say, "it won't be for the right reasons."

Ren takes a sip of his red wine, watches me for several steady moments before he says, "What is his reason?"

"Guilt?" My answer is automatic and uncensored.

"Because he didn't come with you in the first place?"

I shake my head. "No. That wouldn't have been enough to bring him all the way over here."

"What then?"

I want to change the subject because I honestly don't know if I can answer him without making a bawling fool of myself. But he's watching me with his patient blue gaze, and there's something very like compassion there. And it's only then that I realize how much I need to talk about it. If for no other reason than to provide a release valve for the pressure that's been building inside me since Winn's phone call.

"As it turns out, my best friend discovered the real reason Ty didn't want to come on this trip with me."

Ren says nothing, just continues to wait with that steady gaze of his, as if he has all the time in the world and is willing to give it to me if that's what it takes for me to finish what I've started.

"It's cliché to the point of being embarrassing."

"Go on," he says.

I try to. My lips actually part with the words' intent to come out. Only I can't make them. And I sit there with my fork poised in midair, mute, while tears well in my eyes and glide down my cheeks. He slides his chair back, stands and walks around the table to sit next to me.

He slips an arm around my shoulder and pulls me up close against him. My resistance lasts for no more than a second, and I literally crumple into him. He brushes his hand across the back of my hair.

I am mortified to feel myself sobbing into his shoulder. My

sobs have no sound, but my shoulders shake. I don't know how long I cry like that. It doesn't matter. He just lets me. Every once in a while, telling me in a soft voice that I'm okay, that everything will be all right. I don't know how to tell him that it really won't. That seems a little like a slap in the face of his kindness.

So I settle for silence until my crying is spent, and my shoulders go still, and I am finally silent. I have no idea how I am going to make myself pull back and look him in the face. I have no choice, so I force myself to do exactly that. While I'm not sure what I expected to see in his eyes, amusement, ridicule, it's neither. It's just caring. Unmasked. Unhidden. And I realize that I can tell him. That I need to tell him.

"She's a junior partner at his firm. Very pretty. Very smart."

Ren smoothes the back of his hand across my cheek. "And he has no idea what he has in you?"

"Apparently nothing he wants anymore," I say, hoping I don't sound pitiful because I certainly feel pitiful.

"Then that makes him the fool," Ren says, "not you."

I drop my chin, a small laugh of disagreement escaping from my throat. "Not in anyone else's eyes," I say. "Including my own."

With one finger, he tips my chin up, forcing me to look at him. "He is the fool," he says.

I want to believe him. Down to the core of my soul, I want to believe him. Rejection does that to you. Makes you savagely thirsty for reassurance that somewhere down the road, someone might again find you appealing, once the sheen of rejection has lost its glisten. I know, however, that right now, I must positively glow with it.

"I think, Lizzy, that when we betray someone like that, the way you've been betrayed, it says more about something wrong in the person doing the betraying, than it does about the one being betrayed."

I hear conviction in his tone and something else, too, that I can't quite identify. It almost sounds like remorse. And I want to ask him if he's been through the same thing, but even as the thought enters my mind, it strikes me how laughable it would be to think that anyone would cheat on Ren Sawyer.

"You're brave," he says, breaking the silence.

"Desperate, maybe," I say. "Brave, no."

"You could have caved. Given in," he says. "But you didn't."

"Not this time, anyway," I say, leaning my head back against the booth. I stare up at the ceiling and sigh. "This must seem incredibly mundane to you."

"Lizzy, in this life, everyone has problems. They're not all the same, but it doesn't really matter what you do for a living or who you socialize with, there are still problems. And believe it or not, there have been times when I would have taken mundane and asked for the check."

I raise my head and look at him, smiling a little. "Over actresses in five-star hotel swimming pools?" I ask, referencing a photo I had seen during my Internet ramblings of him with a well-known actress who'd had a little too much to drink.

He raises an eyebrow at me and says, "Don't believe everything you see."

"She looked happy."

"Let's just say the hotel wasn't."

"So it was true?"

"Pieces of it," he concedes. "Not the whole thing though. That's usually how it goes."

I nod, hearing the note of acceptance in his voice.

"Want to get out of here?" he asks.

"Yes," I answer, realizing I no longer have an appetite for any of the food left on my plate.

31

Lizzy

OUTSIDE THE RESTAURANT, a group of six or seven college-age guys and girls stand waiting with expectant expressions. I realize immediately they're there for Ren.

"Hey," Ren says, dropping them a nod in a way that says he's used to this. "What's up?"

A girl with long, silky blonde hair steps forward, her eyes wide with pure delight. "We were sure it was you! Oh, my gosh! Would you mind if we ask for your autograph?"

Ren looks at me, apology in his eyes, as he says, "Sure."

The girl holds out a T-shirt and points at a spot on the back. "I can't believe this!" she says, her hands visibly shaking.

Ren smiles at her, and I wonder if he has any idea what kind of effect he has on women. I know he does. But I mean *really*.

All the guys and girls step forward for their turn to get an item signed. Once he finishes, they begin thanking him in unison.

"No problem," Ren says, and then nodding at the guitar case one of the guys is holding, he adds, "Wanna do a couple?"

Everyone in the group looks as if they could be knocked over with a feather, their eyes wide and their nods mute.

One of them pulls the guitar from the case and starts to hand it to Ren, but he says, "You know 'Send Me a Sign'?"

"Yeah," the guy says. "I know it."

They sit down on a nearby stone wall, and he begins picking out the song, warming up a bit and then dipping into the intro.

Ren starts to sing, and I sit down to listen, as rapt as everyone else in the group. Other people start to wander over, and it's not long before a small crowd forms. I hear the murmurings of recognition. But everyone is respectful and appreciative, and for the next hour, they go from one song to another. When Ren indicates it's time to stop, they all clap and whistle. He spends another twenty minutes signing more autographs. Once he's finished, he looks at me and says, "Ready?"

I nod. "That was incredible," I say.

"Thanks," he says, reaching for my hand. And we walk like this all the way back to the hotel, as if it is something we have the right to do.

~

WE TAKE THE STAIRS to our rooms. We stop in front

of my door. I insert the key, but before I can turn the lock, Ren puts his hands on my shoulders and turns me to face him.

"I'm going to tell you something that I have a feeling you're not going to believe because of what you told me earlier."

My eyes lock into his, and I don't think I can make myself look away even if the walls start to fall in around us. "What?" I ask, the word barely audible.

"There's nothing in this world I want more right now than to carry you into this room and make love to you. And not just to prove you wrong about there being something in you that would cause a man to do what your husband did."

I feel the breath catch in my throat, the protest I'm trying to form not even believable to me.

He leans in then and kisses me, softly at first, as if asking permission. And when I open my mouth beneath his, the kiss becomes something completely different. It is a kiss of lust and longing so easily identifiable that even I can't deny his sincerity. And when he pulls me up against him, I know I'm right. I think how amazing it is to be held like this, kissed like this. To feel so wanted. Just that. Wanted and not alone.

I don't know how long we kiss this way, but it's long enough that I'm fairly sure there's a point not too far ahead where turning back isn't going to be an option. Maybe he feels this thought as it shudders through me because he steps back, still connected to me with a hand at my waist. Breathing heavy and hard, he says, "That's what I want to do. But that's not the right thing for you right now."

"I hate sensibility," I say, the words out before I can even think about censoring them.

His smile is the one that's made who knows how many girls fall in love with just that alone. Not having any knowledge of the rest of him, of how decent a man he is. And as much as I foolishly want to toss what he's just said to the wind, I know he's right. For a million reasons, he's right.

Right, however, doesn't equal easy.

I draw in a deep breath, force myself to turn away and finish opening the door. "Good night, Ren," I say.

"Good night, Lizzy."

And I close the door.

32

Ren

I'VE SPENT THE LAST fifteen years of my life pleasing pretty much no one but myself. I've been the kind of guy who sees something he wants and simply takes it if it's offered, regardless of who it might hurt. Even people I've loved most in this world.

So no one could be more shocked by what I just said to Lizzy than I am. It's not that I didn't want to spend the night in her bed. But it would have happened because she's hurting. And I would have been far more of an ass than her husband if I had taken advantage of that.

I pick up Sophia from her snoozing spot on the bed and step out of my room onto the terrace that overlooks a small, very well-kept garden of boxwoods and Italian cypresses. Low lights form a perimeter around it, and I can see at the center a marble statue of a horse and rider.

I wish I could say that what I did just now makes me somebody worth admiring, but it doesn't. I think the truth is I already have to look at myself in the mirror every day and know that the man staring back at me is a man capable of betraying his own brother in the worst kind of way. I am that man, and I could spend the rest of my life making different choices, trying to be someone else, when in the end, I can't erase what I did. Nothing I ever do, no matter how good, how generous, how selfless, will ever make up for that, will ever fix it. It's not fixable. I'm not fixable.

And when something isn't fixable, it's just broken. Maybe that's how I deserve to live the rest of my life. The thought surprises me. I realize it's the first time in three years that I've thought in those terms. The truth is I haven't been thinking of life past the moment when I finally take that bottle out of its hiding place in my shaving case. The moment when I unscrew the lid and take those pills one at a time, every single one, until I am erased from this earth, snuffed out like an insignificant spark whose impact was more flicker than flame.

Sophia whimpers and tries to nestle closer in the bend of my arm. Her eyes are closed, and she's all but asleep. I think of the way she had looked under our car, cowering and shaking as if certain that her fate would not be a kind one. In all reality, it would not have been if we hadn't taken her with us.

I don't know what they do to homeless dogs in Italy, but I know what they do in American shelters when a dog isn't wanted or claimed by anyone. And just the thought of someone taking this little life makes me feel physically sick.

I sit down on a chair near the railing, lean back with my legs stretched out in front of me. Sophia wiggles up my chest to lay her head on my shoulder like a newborn baby. I feel a surge of something I instantly recognize as love. Pure and overwhelmingly real. At the same time, I think of Lizzy and another tangle of emotion settles over me.

Just a few days ago, I had no desire to remain on this earth. The truth is I knew I didn't deserve to be here any longer. And I still don't if I judge myself for what I did to my own brother. In my decision making, I had taken into account the fact there really wasn't anyone I was sad to leave behind.

Only now there is. A married woman and a little white dog.

33

Lizzy

I FLIP ONTO MY back and throw the covers off for at least the fifth time since I got in bed a couple of hours ago.

I haven't slept. I can't sleep because all I keep thinking about is that kiss Ren left me with at the door.

Somewhere along the line, I don't even know how many years ago, I started to realize that I no longer felt like an attractive woman. It wasn't something that hit me in one fell swoop of acceptance, but something that seeped into me, little by little, fueled by the fact that Ty rarely noticed my appearance whether I had on sweat pants or a short skirt. Of course, there was also the fact that our sex life had ceased to exist. And I didn't reject the theory that I was simply no longer attractive to him. I think on some level I accepted it as one of those truths of life. That whatever had made me attractive to him in college, when we were first married, I didn't have any more. For him, or for anyone.

But standing outside this room, in the arms of a man I didn't even know a week ago, I wonder if maybe I was wrong. Could it be that Ren really had wanted me, and the only reason he had left was conscience? Lying here in the dark, thinking these thoughts, I have to admit that maybe I wish his conscience hadn't made itself known until the morning. But no sooner have I released the thought than I can't deny that he was right.

I rub my bare wedding-ring finger. Even though I've removed the ring, I'm still married. I have no right to Ren. Because despite anything he might offer me as solace to a very bruised ego, I'm still married. In actuality, I should have been the one turning him away, listening to conscience. In another phase of my life, a time when I hadn't felt so rejected, I would have, because regardless of how Ty and I started out, the bond of marriage and the vows I made have always meant something to me.

I once thought they meant something to Ty.

The thought of facing him, of hashing out everything that will have to be hashed out between us, makes me feel sick.

I don't want to hear his whys and his explanations and justifications for the choice he made. Ty is a lawyer. He convinces for a living. Somehow, someway he will convince me that his choice was entirely my fault. That I'm really the one to blame for the fact that he jilted our anniversary trip in favor of a twenty-four-year-old attorney.

A rap at the door bolts me off the bed. My stomach plummets at the very same moment, and I am suddenly drenched in a confused combination of heat and cold. Has Ren changed his mind? Have I changed mine? I don't have an answer to either of those questions.

But I get up and walk to the door anyway, turning the dead bolt lock only to find that it is not Ren standing on the other side.

It's Ty.

I picture myself as I know I must look. Eyes wide and still hazy with lustful thoughts of another man. Lips parted in complete and utter surprise.

"Hey," he says, not angry, as I might have expected, but contrite.

Contrite is something Ty has never done. It's as unnatural to him as accepting defeat without an all-out brawl to the death.

For the life of me, I cannot speak. I try to force his name past my lips, but it won't come. It is stuck somewhere in the back of my throat behind a scream of utter outrage for the fact that he has caught me so off guard.

"May I come in?" he asks, and I notice immediately how tired he looks. His white cotton shirt is uncharacteristically wrinkled and untucked from his khaki pants.

"Um, no," I say. "As a matter of fact, you can't."

His eyes widen almost imperceptibly, and if I didn't know him so well I might have missed it. But I do know him, and he did not expect my answer.

"What do you mean, I can't come in?" he asks evenly. "I'm your husband."

The laugh leaves my throat before I realize it's even there. And it is funny, actually, the irony of it.

"So you do remember that?" I ask, once my amusement has faded.

"Let me come in, Lizzy. We need to talk."

"Well, see, I don't really think we need to talk. I think I know everything I need to know."

He doesn't answer right away. "Lizzy, it's not—"

"Yes, it is," I say. "It *so* is."

The words slip out, so revealing, so indicative of my hurt, I want to grab them back, hide my pain from him, and not give him the satisfaction of knowing what he has done to me.

He reaches out and pulls me hard up against him with one arm, while anchoring his other hand in the back of my hair. He leans in and kisses me fast and furious, and the first thing that registers is, this is how he used to kiss me. Before I became neutral in his eyes. Before whatever he used to see in me faded away.

For whatever reason, the tables have now turned, and Ty is seeking instead of rejecting. I allow this to have its effect, feeling just the smallest amount of gratification. And then I realize how much I do not want him to kiss me. I try to pull away, but he's not letting me, and I push against his chest saying, "Stop, Ty. Stop!"

"You don't really want me to," he says. "You want me to

come in there and beg for forgiveness, and I can do that. I will do that. Let me, Lizzy," he says and kisses me again.

This time I catch him slightly off guard. When I push him away, he stumbles back a bit and hits the corner of a table against the wall behind him. He kicks the table and then, "Damn it, Lizzy. What are you doing?"

"Leave, Ty. I want you to leave."

I hear the chain on the door to the room next to mine. It is only then that it occurs to me we might wake up Ren. The door opens, and there he stands, shirtless, in jeans and bare feet.

"Are you okay, Lizzy?"

"Yes," I say, my voice shaking a little.

Ty looks from me to Ren and then back at me again. "What the hell is going on here?" He starts to say something, and then stops as if the words won't come out. Finally, he manages, "Are you telling me that the two of you have been—"

He breaks off and takes a step back, raking a hand through his hair and anchoring the other on his hip. He stares at us both in utter shock.

"It's not what you think," I say.

"Then what the hell is it?" he says, each word measured and tight, barely concealing his anger. He looks back at Ren, and I see the moment of recognition on his face. It's quickly followed by disbelief.

"I'm a friend of Lizzy's," Ren says. "That's who I am. And if she doesn't want you here, you need to go."

Ty shakes his head as if he has no idea where to go from there. He laughs a short laugh and looks at me, saying, "So I came over here thinking I was the bad guy, all prepared to do anything to get you to forgive me. And as it turns out, you must have been hoping I would back out of the trip." He stares at me and then at Ren and says, "Although this makes absolutely no sense."

"Which part?" Ren asks, his voice low and careful.

"The part where my wife has been screwing a rock star."

The punch is so quick and so sudden that I can't quite believe it's really happened until Ty is picking himself up off the floor and coming at Ren with the look of a bull that just discovered a competitor in his pasture. He charges at Ren, knocking him into the open doorway of the room. They both stumble through, and I scream for them to stop. The room is dark, and I can barely make out who is who. But I hear punches. I also hear Sophia whimper from somewhere in a corner of the room, and now I am yelling. "Stop, stop, stop!"

The room goes silent. I flick on the hallway light, spot Sophia huddled by the nightstand and run over to scoop her up.

A hotel manager is now standing in the doorway, looking as if he's not sure whether to come in or run.

"What is going on here?" he asks, in an authoritative voice.

"Everything is fine," I say. "Just a misunderstanding."

The manager looks from Ren to Ty, shakes his head and says, "Must I call the *polizia*?"

"No, no," I say, pleading in my voice. "Everything is okay." I point at Ty. "But this man isn't staying at the hotel. Could you please ask him to leave?"

"Lizzy!" Ty barks.

"Go, Ty. This isn't how we're going to solve anything."

"I think it's pretty clear that you're not looking to solve anything with me," Ty says.

"I believe she asked you to leave," Ren says.

Ty shakes his head as if he has no idea what to make of any of it. And for a moment I almost feel sorry for him. Maybe I do feel sorry for the old Ty. Just not for the new one.

He turns abruptly and walks out of the room, slamming the door shut behind him. The strip of moon through the balcony door is the only light left. Even so, I can feel Ren's gaze on me.

Sophia wiggles in my arms. I reach out and hand her to him.

"Are you okay?" he asks, his voice quiet and soft.

I nod. "I should be asking you."

He rubs his palm across the left side of his face. "He's got a decent right hook. I'll give him that."

"I'm so sorry to have dragged you into this," I say, mortification beginning to set in.

He shrugs. "Don't be."

A large red circle is beginning to imprint on his left cheek. I reach out and touch it with one finger, then quickly pull back as if the touch has just burned me.

"That's going to hurt. Do you want me to get some ice?"

"No. It'll be fine. I've had worse, believe me."

"I wouldn't have taken you for the brawling type."

He smiles. "I usually try avoidance as a tactic whenever possible. Saves the knuckles."

We study each other for a moment. At least a dozen things I should probably say cross my mind. I reject each of them though under the painful awareness that what has just happened will change things. I can no longer go gallivanting all over Tuscany pretending that I don't have a situation in my life that needs resolving. Clearly, it does, and no one else can do that for me. Not Winn by giving me a heads-up. Or Ren by coming to my defense with his fists.

Tomorrow I will face the music as I already should have done. If I had, none of this would have happened tonight. All I want to do now is sleep and hope that when I wake up tomorrow, things will look a little better than they do now. I'm not sure how that will happen, considering where things stand at this moment, but I guess I can hope.

"If you're sure you're okay, I think I'm going to bed."

"Okay," he says.

I take a step back and start to turn toward my door when he says, "Lizzy?"

I turn back. "Yes?"

"Are you sure you're all right?" he asks.

I can't deny the concern in his voice, and I wish I could wrap myself up in it like a cocoon of comfort. But I just say, "I'm good. See you in the morning, okay?"

"Good night, Lizzy," he says, and with obvious reluctance, leaves.

34

Kylie

KYLIE COMES AWAKE abruptly.

Her eyes fly open, and she instantly flashes to the last thing she remembers. A hand with some kind of cloth covering her face, a smell that she fights but fails to push away. She could only breathe it in, and then nothing.

Until now.

She tries to scoot up, but finds that her hands are locked behind her back, chained to something—a bed rail. She yanks at it, feels her shoulder scream in protest. She cries out in frustration, looking around in panic at her surroundings.

The floor is some kind of yellowed linoleum. Black paper has been stapled to the windows, and the only light is what seeps in around the seams.

"Hey. Are you awake?"

The girl's voice makes Kylie scream. Only her scream is

muffled by the tape across her mouth. She makes a sound to indicate yes.

"Good. I've been trying to wake you up for hours."

Kylie tries to ask where she is, but the sounds behind the tape do not come out as words.

"Don't try to talk. They won't take off the tape until you quit trying to scream. I'm over here, on the other side of the bed. I've been here three days, and I'm sorry that you're here, too, but I've never been so glad to see another human being as I was to see you."

Kylie tries to scream, "Why?"

"They haven't done anything to me yet. I think they're planning to take us somewhere. I overheard one of them say they needed two more after me. So I guess we'll be waiting until they get another one."

Another one? Kylie hears herself being described as a thing, and she is suddenly so filled with rage that she starts to buck against the chain holding her hands prisoner. This can't be happening! This CANNOT be happening!

"You'll just hurt yourself," the girl says, her words underlined with the acceptance of defeat. "I've tried all of it. You won't get loose."

But Kylie isn't a quitter. She twists and pulls until her joints scream in protest, and she is sobbing behind the tape.

Her efforts do not go unnoticed. A key sounds in the lock of the door across from the bed. A large man walks in, holding a rag in his hand. Kylie looks at his face and realizes he's wearing a mask, the face of an old man with stringy gray hair.

She starts to sob, but the cries stall in her throat.

The rag covers her nose, and she tries to hold her breath. But the man is patient and waits until she can no longer refuse. She breathes in with the panic of suffocation and everything around her falls away.

35

Lizzy

I OPEN MY EYES to pounding. At first, I think it's a hammer. But as my grogginess starts to lift, I realize someone is knocking at my door.

"*Signora* Harper?"

I throw my legs over the side of the bed, stand and walk in a not-so-steady path to the door. I look through the peephole and see the manager from last night wearing a very worried look on his face. I open the door just far enough to peer out and say, "Yes?"

"I am very sorry to disturb you, *signora*. But I have had a phone call this morning, a most troubling phone call."

"What is it?" I ask, suddenly worried.

"The polizia are asking about the incident last evening."

For a moment I have to wonder what incident and then the memory of what had happened in the hallway between

Ty and Ren washes over me. And right behind it, a sweep of anxiety.

"What did they want?"

"It would seem *Signore* Harper is filing charges against *Signore* Sawyer."

"What?" The question comes out on a gasp of disbelief.

"*Si, si.* I thought you might want to know. The *polizia* are on their way just now."

"Now?"

"*Si.* I did not know if you might wish to leave." He lifts his shoulders in a shrug. "If you would like to go, I will tell them I am not aware of your leaving."

My mind is suddenly so full of anger at Ty that I can barely force myself to speak.

"You are very kind. I will speak to *Signore* Sawyer. But what about our bill?" I ask, shaking my head.

"Is fine," he says. "Come again another time."

"But we can't possibly—"

"You should leave, *signora*," he says in a more serious tone. "I feel the paparazzi will be not far behind the *polizia*."

I realize then that he is fully aware of who Ren is, and this act of kindness is one I shouldn't question.

"Thank you," I say, grateful. "Thank you so much."

I close the door, grab a pair of jeans and a T-shirt and yank them on as fast as I have ever gotten dressed in my life. I slip on sandals, toss the rest of my belongings in my open suitcase, pack up my laptop and camera and drag them quickly out the door. At Ren's room, I rap quickly and sharply and call his name a few times before he comes to the door, looking ridiculously appealing considering that I have just woken him up.

"Hey," he says, running a hand through his dark wavy hair.

"I think we have to go."

He raises his eyebrows and says, "What do you mean, have to go?"

"The manager just came up to warn me that the police have called. Ty has apparently filed charges against you. He suggested we go."

Ren stares at me for several long seconds as if he's not sure what to say.

"I don't generally run from guys like Ty," he says carefully. "And he threw the first punch."

"Do you want to stay and explain that to them?"

"We can." He shrugs. "I'm good either way."

But I see the awareness on his face of exactly what being questioned by the Italian police will mean for him. A scene he would no doubt rather avoid. Press he would no doubt rather avoid.

"Let's go," I say.

"Are you sure?"

"Yes."

"Can you get Sophia? I'll grab my things."

I leave my bag in the hallway, step into the room and walk to the bed where the tiny dog is curled up on a pillow. She had apparently been asleep next to Ren. I wait with her in the hallway, and it's ninety seconds or less before Ren comes out and closes the door behind him.

"We should go by the front desk and settle up," he says.

"I don't think there's time, and the manager was kind enough to say it would be okay to go. He said the paparazzi would not be far behind."

I see the gratitude on his face as he nods and says, "Okay, let's get out of here."

He grabs my suitcase, and I tuck Sophia under my arm. We take the stairs and when we reach the bottom I say, "It would seem we're making a habit of this."

"It would seem," he says.

We all but sprint to the car, and this time he says, "I'll drive."

I hand him the keys and get in the passenger side.

Sophia is trying to wriggle out of my arms, and I suspect that she has to go potty.

"We'll stop a few miles from here," Ren says, throwing the car into gear. We take the road behind the hotel. It's steep and winding and narrow enough that I'm hoping we don't meet another car. Luckily, we don't. When we hit the paved road, Ren winds out the Fiat's small engine.

Neither one of us says anything for the next ten minutes. The sun is just starting to come up as he pulls onto a gravel turnoff and eases the car into the grass at the edge of the road. We both get out and let Sophia take care of business. Within two minutes, we're back in the car driving. We say nothing, but my mind is racing to find a solution to fix this. Ren's face is solemn and serious in a way I don't think I've seen in him so far. The realization prompts me to say, "Why don't we go back? Surely, they will understand once we explain."

But he stops me with, "I need to make a call. It won't take very long."

He finds another place to turn and pulls far enough off the main road that we won't be seen by anyone driving by. He gets out and walks a short way from the car, pulling his phone from his pocket and tapping the screen. He's pacing while he waits, the phone to his ear. He starts to talk, although I can't understand what he's saying. It's brief. He gets back in the car, and we drive off again.

"Is everything all right?" I ask.

"That was my manager. He's looking for somewhere out of the way where we can go for a bit. He'll call back in a few minutes."

I start to say something but realize that I have no idea what to say. I'm beginning to realize that we might both be in a lot of trouble.

"Let me just call Ty," I say. "I can smooth this out."

He glances at me and says, "How?"

"By telling him I'll come home."

And even as the words come out, I feel this incredible weight of sadness settle around me. "It's what I need to do anyway. At some point, I'll have to face the music. It might as well be now."

He looks at me, one hand on the steering wheel. "That might be, but not like this."

I start to argue, but I can't seem to force the words past my lips. The thought of leaving this incredible place, of never seeing Ren again makes me feel as if I can't get a full breath. I know I should argue and do exactly what I just suggested, but I don't want to. And so I press my lips together and stare out the window at the Italian countryside rolling by.

Several minutes pass before Ren's phone rings. He picks it up, swipes the screen. "Hey." He listens for a few moments and then says, "Can you text me the address? Okay," he adds. "Thanks, Stuart. I'll be in touch."

He ends the call and glances at me. "There's a place a couple of hours away from where we are now. My," he hesitates, "manager says we won't be found there."

"Ah," I say, nodding as if I understand a world where I could make a single phone call and have someone arrange an out-of-the-way place in another country where I could have complete privacy.

"You're good with it?" he asks.

I nod. Even though every part of me is questioning whether we should just go back and fix this mess before it gets completely out of control. His phone dings, indicating the text has arrived. He opens it, glances at the address and then asks me to type it into his GPS. I do, even though my fingers are shaking, and I wonder how this can possibly be a good idea.

We arrive at the turnoff almost two hours later. Sophia stands with her tiny front paws on my window ledge looking out, her little tail wagging. Ren looks at her with a half-smile.

"At least one of us is happy about this."

We follow the gravel road for at least a mile. It's narrow and winding and covered in places with small brown pea gravel, bare in others.

The road dips and turns, and suddenly a very large Tuscan villa comes into view.

"What is the name of the hotel?" I ask.

Without looking at me, Ren says, "It's actually a private home. It's been available for rent. Stuart says it's for sale. So actually, there's no one here."

My hesitation must be transparent because he instantly says, "Bad idea?"

For so many reasons I think, and then quickly regain traction with, "It's beautiful," I say.

"I'll put you on one end and me on the other," he offers, as if he has read my thoughts.

From any stance of common sense, it is the only plan I should even think of agreeing to. Why then the wave of disappointment?

The villa sits in a scoop of valley, gentle hills rolling out from each side. It is old and extremely well-kept. The walls are that beautiful Tuscan gold color, the roof terra-cotta tile. Enormous Italian cypress trees grace the front and corners of the villa.

"It looks like a place where a Medici might have lived," I say. "How did your manager find this in such a short amount of time?"

"That's what he does. He takes care of things, and he's really good at it."

"Apparently," I say.

"And two," Ren says, "he had the added motivation of wanting to keep me out of trouble. I suspect he knew that's where I was headed.

"Is that a regular occurrence?" I ask.

"Not nearly as often as it used to be," he says, a half-smile on his ridiculously beautiful mouth. He pulls the Fiat to a stop in the circular driveway, stopping just short of the museum-size front door.

"The caretaker is supposed to meet us here," he says.

We get out of the car, Sophia wide-eyed in my arms. I think she's as awed by the place as I am. Just then a man with graying hair and a welcoming smile appears from one side of the villa.

"*Buon giorno!*" he says lifting a hand in welcome. "You are *Signore* Sawyer?"

"Yes," Ren says, stepping forward to shake the man's hand.

"I am Antonio. I will be happy to escort you in and show you the place."

"Thank you. That would be great," Ren says.

Antonio opens the door for us, then steps aside and lets us precede him into the foyer of the house. All words leave me. The walls are fresco scenes of Italian life in times past. There's one of the sea on our right, and to our left a sprawling vineyard. A travertine staircase winds from this floor to the next. The ceilings are fifteen feet by my best guess, and it's hard to believe this is a private residence.

"We will cover the basics, no?" says Antonio.

Ren nods. "Sure. After you."

We follow him down a long hall to the kitchen area.

"The most important, yes?" says Antonio.

I smile and say, "It would be for me, if I could cook the way you cook in Italy."

"Ah, it is practice and the right ingredients," Antonio says modestly. "Fresh, of course, and local."

The kitchen is a charming mixture of the past and the present. Stone counter tops and terra-cotta tile flooring are smoothly worn with centuries of use. In direct contrast, a gleaming Viking stove that might be featured in a five-star restaurant takes up half of one wall. Copper pots hang from a rack above, some big enough to feed dozens. A wine refrigerator sits next to a stainless-steel Viking refrigerator, again big enough to be used in the most professional of restaurants. He leads us out of the kitchen onto an expansive terrace with stone walls and a covered summer kitchen. A pool stretches out from the right corner, turquoise and inviting.

"Is very nice this time of year," Antonio says, pointing at it. "And not to worry, your privacy is complete."

Heat strikes my cheeks as soon as the words have left his mouth, and I cannot bring myself to look at Ren. Sophia is begging to be put down so I set her on the stone floor, a handy excuse to avoid Ren's amused gaze. Sophia yips and trots off ahead of us, inspecting as she goes.

"I will show you upstairs now," Antonio says.

We follow him back through the kitchen and down the corridor to the stairs at the front of the villa. At the top, Sophia races by us, stopping to see which way Antonio will go. When he turns right, she zips ahead again down the long hallway, the walls of which feature paintings of scenic Tuscan hills and vineyards and olive groves.

We pass at least six doors that I assume are bedrooms, finally arriving at one where Antonio stops. He turns the knob and opens the door to the bedroom, which is actually a suite of rooms. A living area to the left is complete with a large screen TV and four comfy red sofas.

Farther in, glass-pane doors open to a bedroom, the center of which holds a giant king-size bed with an oversized carved walnut headboard. Sophia attempts a leap but manages to hit only halfway up. She lands on her backside with a thud. Ren immediately scoops her up and soothes her bruised ego before depositing her on the bed.

"Is there anything else I can do for you, *Signor* Sawyer?"

"No, thank you, Antonio."

"Very good then, my number is on the desk in the foyer. If you need anything, do not hesitate to call."

Ren hands him a folded bill and says, "Thank you very much."

Antonio leaves the room, and it is only then that I fully

realize it has been assumed this room is for the two of us. I look at Ren. He is looking at me.

"Awkward," I say.

"Don't worry," he says. "I can sleep anywhere."

"No, you take this room. I'll find another."

"Stay," he says. "I'll go get the luggage. You're here, I'm elsewhere."

I want to argue but I can tell by the look on his face that it will do absolutely no good.

He leaves the room, and I stand there for a moment feeling like Alice in Wonderland. I flop back first onto the bed, arms and legs splayed, staring at the ceiling.

What am I doing here? I know Ty, and if last night left him angry enough to go to the Italian police and file a complaint, I can only imagine what he will do if he finds out that I have fled the scene with Ren and am hiding out in an Italian villa. It's not like that, but I guess it would appear like that. My hope is to simply give him time to cool off and change his mind about trying to have the last word. Ren appears in the doorway then with my suitcase, laptop and camera bag.

"Did someone call for a porter?" he says.

I vault off the bed, walk over and take two of the bags from him.

He puts my suitcase in the closet, then turns to look at me.

"The pool looked inviting. Are you up for it?"

I do have a swimsuit, but the thought of putting it on and actually wearing it in front of Ren is enough to make me plead a headache and a need for an afternoon nap. "Oh, I don't know, I'm really not much of—"

"Come on," he says. "It'll be fun. I'm sure they have extra suits here if you need one."

"I have one. As well as a coverup," I add under my breath.

"What was that?"

"Nothing."

"Okay, well, I'll see you downstairs in fifteen minutes?"

"Sure."

Sophia dive-bombs off the bed and follows him from the room, her tail a cotton-ball blur. I watch them go and then close the door behind them.

I honestly do not think I can make myself put on that bathing suit and actually wear it in front of him. I picture Gretchen Macher as she had looked on the cover of *Sports Illustrated* last year, another by-product of my Google searching. And I nearly wilt at my own mental comparison. Ah well, that's what coverups are for, and mine will be staying on.

36

Ren

SOPHIA AND I beat Lizzy to the pool. I will actually be surprised if she comes at all, considering that her reluctance to agree could not have been more obvious. I throw a towel across a chair at one end of the pool, stretch out face down, running my hand through the warm blue water. I hear her sandals on the stone floor and look up. She looks as if she would rather be anywhere else in the world. With the benefit of my sunglasses I start to say something, but then my gaze snags on her long tan legs, and I take advantage of my sunglasses to admire them a moment or two longer. I rise up on my elbows and say, "Hey, you came."

"I did," she says.

I get up and pull a chair next to mine. She sits down, coverup securely in place. I look over at her, raise an eyebrow, "Aren't you a little warm in that?"

"No, actually, I was just thinking it's a bit chilly out here."

I pick up my phone, tap the weather app and show her the screen. 83 degrees.

"Oh, well, maybe I'll warm up in a bit."

"You can't swim in a coverup."

"Who says I'm swimming?"

"I do," I say. I stand, reach for her hand and pull her up from the chair. "Either take it off, or you're going in with it."

"You wouldn't dare."

"Five seconds. Four, three, two—" When she shows no signs of removing it, I pick her up, walk to the deep end of the pool. She's beating at my chest and kicking. Sophia is now running after us and barking.

"Last chance," I say, sticking one foot over the edge of the pool.

"Ren!"

I step off, and we both slice through the water. I hold onto her all the way down and all the way back up. When we cut through the surface, she's sputtering, and to my surprise, I'm smiling.

"I can NOT believe you did that!"

"I did give you fair warning."

The coverup now clings to her curves, and I have no idea why she doesn't want to be seen in a bathing suit. She pushes off my chest and starts to swim away. I reach out and grab her foot and reel her back in. I snag an arm around her waist and get us both to a point where I can stand, all the while not letting her go. There is no denying my awareness of her. I can see it on her face, the way it makes her lips go slightly slack and deepens the color of her eyes.

"What are we doing, Lizzy?" I ask, my voice barely audible.

She stares up at me for several long heartbeats before saying, "Being foolish?"

I shake my head. "I don't feel foolish." I reach out and trace my finger along the edge of her jaw.

"What do you feel, then?"

"Like I found something I never knew I was looking for, and now that I know it exists, the thought of letting it go, feels like a great big hole in the center of me."

She starts to say something, presses her lips together and then begins again. "This isn't real, Ren. People like you and me don't do things like this."

"Like what?"

"Step outside of their real lives and be something else."

"Do you think we're not being ourselves?"

"No, I don't think we are."

"I think you're wrong about that. I think maybe we've both figured out that there's another way to live."

"But there isn't," she says. She puts her palms against my chest and tries to push away.

"There is," I say. "I think you've shown me that."

She shakes her head. "Don't Ren, don't. This is . . . don't. You can't do this."

"Do what?"

"Pretend that this can go somewhere."

"Why can't it?" I ask.

"Because," she says, dropping her head back and staring up at the sky.

I hear the slightest sigh escape her lips and I know I'm not wrong about what's between us.

"I don't think you have any idea how different our lives are," she says.

I take her hand; lead her to the shallow end of the pool. I lift her up and set her on the side, standing in front of her, one arm on either side of her hips.

"You have no idea," I say, "what you've done for me, Lizzy."

She's fully focused on me, confusion clear in her eyes.

"When I boarded that flight out of the U.S., I didn't intend to ever return."

"What do you mean?" she asks carefully.

"I mean—" I stop because the words are too hard to say.

"What?" she asks, and I hear the concern in her voice. She puts two fingers under my chin and forces me to look at her. "Tell me."

"I didn't want to live that life anymore."

"You wanted to quit your music?"

I don't answer for several moments, and then, "I wanted to quit my life." Hearing myself say it out loud feels like a punch to the stomach.

I see the shock settle onto her face. She starts to say something, then stops and shakes her head.

"Why would you . . . Ren, why?"

I get out of the pool, sit on the edge next to her, my palms braced on either side of me. I don't say anything for a good while, and when I do, I hear the shame in my voice. "I've done some pretty awful things, Lizzy."

"Everyone makes mistakes, Ren."

"Yeah," I say, and I hear the word break in half. "But does everyone cause their own brother's death?"

I cannot look at her. I feel her looking at me, and I can no more turn my face to hers than I can remove this lead weight from my chest. She places her left hand over my right, links our fingers together as if she feels a sudden need to anchor me.

"You could never do that."

"I did," I say.

"What?" she asks, shaking her head.

I've never told anyone else in my life what happened that weekend. But I need to now in a way that I cannot turn away from. I am fully aware that in doing so, I might open her eyes to a man she wants nothing to do with. But I need to know more than I need to breathe right now, whether this fallen version of me is a man she could ever accept.

"I loved my brother, Lizzy," I say. "I loved him, but I killed him."

37

Lizzy

I HEAR THE WORDS and yet they make absolutely no sense to me, like letters that have been switched to make sounds I've never heard before.

"But his death was an accident. I read about the bus crash."

He looks up at me, and I have never seen deeper regret than what I see in his blue eyes right now.

"It should have been me," he says. "I should have been on that bus in that seat. Colby was sitting in my seat because I wasn't there. And our drummer was sitting in Colby's regular seat. He was fine."

"Ren, you can't—"

"I can," he interrupts me. "I can." His voice slices through my protest. "You remember how I told you I wasn't a very good guy?"

"I know you said that," I say. "But I don't believe it."

"I didn't get on the bus that day. I was supposed to. Colby's fiancee asked me not to. She said she had something she wanted to talk to me about. I knew on some level what she wanted. We used to date, and a couple of years after we broke up, she and Colby started dating. I should never have stayed behind that night. If I hadn't, he would be here, and I wouldn't."

"Ren, you don't know that."

"I loved my brother," he says, his voice hardly recognizable, "and if it weren't for me—"

"Stop," I say softly. "Stop." I slip my arms around his neck and pull him to me. I can feel how close he is to breaking, and I want nothing more in this world than to hold him together. I lean back and press my hand to the side of his face.

He looks at me, and I honestly feel as if I could drown in his sorrow.

"You didn't mean for him to die, Ren."

"No," he says. "I just wish it had been me instead of him."

38

Ren

WE SIT AT the pool for most of the afternoon. We talk very little, but somehow I don't need that with her. Just having her next to me is enough.

Lizzy isn't judging me. I feel that, and I'm grateful for it. Undeserving of it, but grateful.

We agree to meet downstairs for dinner around seven. After I go upstairs and change, I head out for a run. I'm not sure how long I'm out there or how far I go. But I run full out as if something in the effort can leech from me the guilt that's become part of my every breath, every heartbeat.

I run until I have to stop and bend over at the knees, pulling in air, my lungs frantic for the next gulp of oxygen. I'm almost back to the villa when my phone rings. I glance at the screen, see that it's Stuart and consider not answering. But I know I owe him for finding this place so quickly, so I do.

"Have you seen the news?" he snaps.

And I know this is not going to be pleasant. "No," I say. "I haven't."

"Well, you've made entertainment headlines."

I want to tell him I couldn't care less, but I can hear in his voice he's going to tell me, anyway.

"Who is she?"

"She?" I keep the question neutral.

"The woman whose picture is splattered all over *Entertainment Nightly*. I'm assuming she's the reason you needed a place to hide out."

"It's not like that, Stuart."

"What is it like, Ren? They're saying you beat the crap out of her husband."

"It wasn't like that, either."

"Then exactly what was it like?" he asks, his voice starting to rise. "Apparently, he's filing charges against you."

"Apparently," I agree.

"Is that what you were running from?"

"I'm not running."

"It looks like running. Just so you know, the headlines are pretty ugly."

"You should know by now that I don't give a damn about the headlines."

"Headlines are one thing. Assault charges another. This is serious. They've been calling me here in New York. Pictures of you two are surfacing in some town called San Gimignano. Look, I don't care who you have an affair with, Ren, but the legal stuff you don't need."

"We're not having an affair," I say.

"It sure looks like it from here."

"Good-bye, Stuart."

"Ren!"

I click off before another word floats up from my phone. I walk back to the villa, go upstairs and stand under a cool shower for ten minutes. With the pounding of the spray comes clarity.

I have to let her go. Home to either fix her life or change it.

39

Ty

YOU OPEN YOUR eyes to bright sunlight trying to break through the heavy curtain of the hotel room. You squint against the light that is successful at penetrating.

You rise up on one elbow, try to make out the numbers on the clock beside the bed, only to discover it's already the middle of the afternoon. You start to sit up, then groan when your face remembers the pain in your jaw. You cup a hand to the swollen spot, trying not to wince at the throbbing.

Damn it all to hell.

You throw your legs over the side of the bed and walk to the bathroom, rummaging through your overnight case in search of some Advil. You find the bottle, dump out two and then swallow them with a glass of water.

You stand with your palms planted on the edge of the sink, forcing yourself to assess the damage to your face in the mirror. Your left eyelid is swollen and starting to turn purple. Your fists clench automatically. You wish you could have another shot at that asshole and his way-too-perfect face.

You wonder what his agenda is. He has to have one. What other reason could he possibly have for being with Lizzy?

You've seen pictures of him in magazines with models, actresses, other singers. Lizzy? A housewife from Virginia?

You spend your days trying to arrange events into patterns of logic. But there is no pattern to be found here.

Lizzy is pretty. You're not blind to that fact. Or, at least, at one time you thought so. But is she in a league with the kind of women Sawyer is usually seen with? No.

What then is his motivation?

You walk back to the bedroom, sit down on the side of the bed and lean forward with your head in your hands.

Does it even matter? Do you even care?

Some part of you does. You can't deny it. You're just not sure which part. The you who married her. Or the you who imagines being the laughingstock among your friends.

Lizzy leaving you for a rock star?

You're pretty sure that as a teenager Kylie had a poster of Sawyer hanging on her bedroom wall after going to one of his concerts. That's some irony.

You're beginning to wonder if you ever should have involved the police. What if it gets in the papers? Shows up back home?

Your face heats up with embarrassment, even at the thought of it.

Should you drop the charges? The idea of letting him off the hook burns like acid in your gut.

But then you wouldn't be doing it for him. You'd be doing it for yourself.

Just as you're about to dial the number left with you by the Italian police, your phone rings. The screen reads Unknown Number. You answer with a cautious, "Hello."

"Mr. Harper?"

"Yes?"

"It's Peyton Kinley. Kylie's roommate."

You can hear now that her voice is shaking. Your heart starts to pound. "Yes, Peyton. What is it?"

"I found your contact info on Kylie's computer. Mr. Harper, I don't know how to tell you this, but Kylie . . . we can't find her. No one knows where she is."

For a moment, the words refuse to penetrate, and you can't bring yourself to respond.

"Mr. Harper?"

"What do you mean no one can find her, Peyton?"

"We went to a bar to see a band. She never came home. I went home for the day, and when I got back, I could tell she hadn't been in the room."

"Are you sure?" you ask, hearing the sharp edges in your voice.

Peyton starts to cry. "Yes, Mr. Harper. I'm sure. I've been asking around, and she wasn't in her classes today. No one has seen her."

"Have you called the police yet?"

"No. I haven't told anyone. I wanted to check with you first."

You force calm into your voice when you say, "Peyton. Listen to me carefully. I want you to call the campus police and report her as missing. I'll call the Charlottesville police and do the same. I'll give them your phone number so they can get in touch with you. I'm in Italy right now, but I'll catch the first available flight back. I imagine D.C. will be the best I can do, and then I'll drive to Charlottesville from there."

"I'm so sorry, Mr. Harper," Peyton says, her sobs now nearly eclipsing her words. "I really don't know where she could be."

"Did she leave the bar with anyone?"

Silence hangs on the line, and then, "The singer from the band, I think. But they've already left town."

"Tell the police everything you know, Peyton. Everything. Do you understand?"

"Yes, sir."

"I'll check in with you as often as I can. If there's any news, please call me and leave a message if I don't answer."

"I will."

You hang up, feeling as if you've taken a right hook to the center of your chest. You sit for a moment and try to organize your thoughts, figure out what is best to do first. And then you just start moving, one action in front of the other. Open your laptop. Find the number for the Charlottesville police department. Call. Wait impatiently until you're put through to a woman who takes your information—what little you have to give her. You tell her you're out of the country and that you'll get back as fast as you can.

It's clear that she's assessing your words, drawing a conclusion perhaps that you're an overprotective father who might be a little too quick to judge a situation that will probably end up being nothing more than a girl taking advantage of freedom.

And so you say, "This is not like my daughter. She doesn't do things like this."

"I'm sure, Mr. Harper. But college kids have a way of proving us wrong."

You end the call, unconvinced that she has taken you seriously. You start to dial the airline and then think about Lizzy.

Should you leave her here and not bother to tell her? But then if this doesn't bring her to her senses, what will? You have no way to get in touch with Lizzy. No idea where she is now. You consider your options. Few come to mind.

But why can't you direct your message to Sawyer? If she's still with him.

You pick up your phone and tap the Twitter icon. In the search bar at the top, you type in his name. Ren Sawyer. Wait to see if he has an account.

Of course he does. You click the Tweet screen and type:

@RenSawyer. May I please have my wife back? Our daughter is missing.

And you Tweet it.

40

Ren

WE ARE OUTSIDE on the terrace, having a glass of wine after dinner. We said very little during the meal, and I think it's because we both know we're at an impasse.

I've been trying to work up my courage for the past two hours, trying to find the words to say what I want to say to her. I line them up in my mind, wanting them to come out as I feel them. But all of a sudden I have the confidence of a teenage boy, and I stumble into the words, awkward and unsure.

"There's something I'd like to say to you, Lizzy."

She sets her wine glass on the wall in front of us, glancing up at me with a look in her eyes that makes me wonder if she wants to hear it.

"Okay," she says.

"I never expected any of this. Meeting you. Spending time together the way we have."

"Neither did I," she agrees quietly.

"But I'm so glad that I did meet you."

"And I'm glad I met you."

"I don't want it to end here."

"I don't want it to end here," she says, reaching out to put her hand over mine. I can feel that she's shaking.

"I'm not asking you to say anything now, Lizzy. We both have loose ends to tie up in our lives if we go anywhere beyond this. Just don't say no to us."

She then lets her gaze meet mine, and I know she's feeling what I'm feeling. It's there in her eyes, undeniable. I brush the back of my hand across her cheek, and lean in and kiss her as I have been wanting to do all day. Her response tells me she's been thinking about it too. And so I slide my arms around her waist, lifting her up onto the wall and stepping in between her legs, pulling her as close as it is possible to do with both of us wearing clothes.

"Ren—" she begins, common sense in her voice, but as soon as I start to pull back, she wraps her arms around my waist and stops me from going anywhere.

We hold onto each other as if we're poised on the edge of a cliff, and we can only save each other by never letting go. And then she's the one kissing me, her hands sliding beneath my T-shirt, up my back, her thumbs tracing my spine. I shiver beneath her touch, dropping my mouth to the side of her neck, my hands sliding her dress off one shoulder so I can kiss the ridge of her collarbone.

She slides my shirt up and over my head, leaning back to study me with a gaze of pure want. She kisses the center of my chest and begins making her way lower, her lips leaving a fire in their wake.

"Lizzy—" I lift her up, cupping her face in my hands. "If you don't stop that, in about sixty seconds, I'll be begging you to come upstairs with me."

"You don't have to beg," she says, rubbing her thumb across my lower lip. "Will you?"

"What?" I ask, the question barely audible.

"Take me upstairs."

"You don't mean it," I say, anchoring my hand in the back of her hair.

"I do mean it," she says, and pulls my mouth back to hers.

I feel the truth in her kiss, and for a little while, I make myself forget everything except what we have right here together.

My phone beeps from its spot on the wall next to us. Lizzy leans away to glance at it, but my phone is the last thing I want to look at right now.

"You have a text," she says, putting her hands against my chest.

"Later," I say, kissing the side of her neck.

"It has exclamation points," she says, picking it up and handing it to me.

I glance at it with reluctance. It's from Stuart.

Check your Twitter account! Now! Please!!

"Is he serious?" I say out loud.

"Looks that way," Lizzy says.

I swipe the screen until I find the Twitter icon that I rarely use. I tap it open and click on Notifications. I scroll through, not seeing anything worthy of Stuart's exclamation points, and then I spot the name Ty Harper and the tweet he'd posted a little over thirty minutes ago.

@RenSawyer May I please have my wife back? Our daughter is missing.

My stomach drops, but I force myself to read it again with skepticism. Based on the Ty Harper I met, I wouldn't put it past him to be making the whole thing up. But then what if he isn't?

"Is everything all right?" Lizzy asks.

"I don't know," I say, wishing I didn't have to show her the message. But I can't keep it from her. I hand her the phone and wait while she reads the tweet from her husband.

"Oh, no," she says softly. "This can't be. I have to call him."

"Of course," I answer. "I'll give you some privacy." I step away and pick Sophia up from her spot on the chair next to Lizzy. I carry her with me into the house, closing the glass-pane door behind us with a quiet click.

41

Lizzy

MY HEART IS BEATING so fast and my hand is shaking so hard that I can barely dial Ty's number. The phone rings five times before he answers with a suspicious, "Hello."

"It's me. What's happened, Ty?"

"Kylie's roommate called. She said Kylie hasn't been back to the room since they went to some club to see a band."

"When was that?"

"About thirty-six hours ago," he says.

"And no one has seen her since then?"

"No."

Panic rises up in a wave. I force myself to try to think. "Have the police been called?"

"I just spoke to someone in Charlottesville. They're looking into it."

"We have to go back," I say.

"I'm booking the next available flight out of Rome. It leaves at seven a.m. Can you make it?"

I have no idea, but somehow I will find a way. I have to. "Yes. Can you text the information to this phone?"

"I'll see you at the airport," he says, and ends the call.

The door opens, and Ren walks out onto the terrace, his dark hair and his tan face drawing my gaze. "Is it true?" he asks.

I nod, unable to hold back the waterfall of tears rushing up and out of me.

He walks over and sits on the wall next to me, putting his arm around my shoulders and pulling me close.

"I have to go," I say.

"I know," he says, kissing my hair.

"My flight is at seven out of Rome."

"I'll get you there."

For a few seconds, and I force myself to count them, I lean into him, draw in his quiet strength, breathe in the scent of him. I never want to forget it or the way it feels when he holds me like this. I try to let each of these things imprint themselves on my memory. I somehow know that once I leave here, that is all I will have to remember him by for the rest of my life.

42

Kylie

SHE'S DEEP, DEEP underwater. Holding her breath, she pushes toward the surface, kicking her legs and propelling her way, up, up, up. She's not sure if she'll be able to hold it long enough to make it all the way to the top.

There's light there. She can see it. She tells herself she can do it. That she has the reserve to make it, keep swimming, keep going. Almost there.

Finally, she breaks through the surface of the light. But it's not water she's broken through. It's consciousness. Her eyes fly open, and panic hits her in a wave.

"Hey," a voice says, and Kylie recognizes it as the girl who is also in the room with her.

"What day is it?" Kylie asks, head throbbing, her mouth so dry she can barely get the words out.

"I'm not sure," the girl says.

"Don't scream," she adds. "Or they'll just come back and knock you out again. It's lonely in here when you're not awake."

Kylie forces herself not to do exactly that, every instinct telling her to scream at the top of her lungs. But she doesn't want to be drugged again. So she keeps her voice low when she says, "What's your name?"

"Erin."

"I'm Kylie," she says.

"Where are you from, Kylie?"

"I go to UVa," Kylie says. "Where are you from?"

"I live about an hour away from Charlottesville. I was walking to the store down the road from my house when this car pulled up behind me, and a guy got out so fast I didn't even realize what was happening until he pushed me inside."

"That's what they did to me too," Kylie says. "Have you heard them say anything else?"

"I think they're planning to sell us," Erin says.

"What?"

"I heard them talking outside the door about how much money they'll get."

And then Kylie remembers what she'd heard them say as well. That they couldn't be damaged.

"This can't be," Kylie says.

"I know. Only on TV. Right?"

"There's got to be some way for us to get out of here." Erin jerks at the cuff on her wrist and shakes her head.

"I've tried."

"I mean later. When they start to take us wherever they're taking us."

"That's probably going to be our only chance," Erin says.

Kylie hears the resignation in her voice, as if she can no longer think about the likely outcome of their situation. But fight flares up inside her, and she tells herself they can't just give up and let themselves be taken somewhere far away where they're probably going to do horrible things to them. Think Kylie, she tells herself.

She knows she has to be smarter than those two thugs. They need a plan. She leans her head back against the bed, closes her eyes and tries to concentrate. She notices she is sitting in some kind of liquid. She looks down, sees the spot on her dress and realizes she has wet herself. It is only then that she begins to cry.

43

Ren

IT TAKES US almost three hours to get to Rome. The traffic is nearly non-existent since we're driving through the night. I drive while Lizzy stares out the window with Sophia curled up on her lap.

Several times, I try to find words that might comfort her. But I don't have any. What can I say that will stop all the scenarios I know must be going through her mind? All the possibilities based on the horrible things we learn about on the news every single day.

At one point, I reach across and take her hand, linking my fingers through hers and holding on tight because I can't think of another single measure of comfort to offer her. And with every mile that slips past on the car's odometer, I feel an approaching sense of loss, like a hole of quicksand in my heart.

I know it's not really possible to lose something that was never really yours, but I feel the loss all the same.

~

LIZZY ASKS IF I will drop her at the terminal in the interest of saving time.

"I'd like to walk you in," I say.

"I appreciate it, Ren, but it's probably better this way."

I know she means that Ty will be waiting inside, and I know that she's right. I nod my okay and drive to the United Airlines dropoff, pulling over and putting the car in park.

We both sit, staring out the windshield, waiting for the other to speak first.

"You're going to blame yourself for what's happening to your daughter, aren't you?"

She bites her lower lip, and then says, "If I hadn't been here, she might have come home, or—"

"Don't do that, okay? Promise me you won't do that."

"Even if it's true?"

"You don't know that."

"I know I've been acting like something I'm not."

"Please don't belittle what we've been to each other here."

"That's not my intention." She hesitates, before adding, "I don't know how to thank you for—"

"You have nothing to thank me for, Lizzy. I'm the one who should be thanking you."

"No," she says, shaking her head. "I think we both needed a friend and just found each other at the right time."

I turn then, wanting to see her face when she answers my next question. "Is that how you see me, Lizzy? As a friend?"

Her eyes fill with tears as she stares back at me. "We both know it can never be more than that."

"Do we?"

She nods, biting her lower lip. "I think I just got caught up in feeling desirable again."

I look into her eyes. "You are desirable. You are desired."

We study each other for several long moments, and it feels as if we're both trying to store away this memory of each other.

"You will never know," she starts.

I reach across and put my thumb to her jaw line, rubbing back and forth. "I know," I say. "I hope you know."

"I do," she says.

I lean in then and kiss her, a whisper of a kiss that lets me taste her tears. She kisses me back, deeper, with open longing and regret. And it's just as I reach for her to pull her closer that she moves away, crying openly now.

She lifts Sophia, kisses her face on both sides and then hands her to me. "I'll get my things from the back," she says.

"Let me help, Lizzy," I say.

"No. Please. It's easier this way."

She gets out of the car, closes the door and quickly opens the hatch, lifting her bags out, and then shuts it. I watch as she walks through the airport's sliding doors. I wait for her to look back, but she doesn't.

44

Lizzy

TY IS WAITING at the ticket counter. Before he spots me, I see him looking at his watch, the impatience that flits across his face.

He looks up then, catches sight of me, leans over and says something to the woman behind the check-in counter. She nods and begins typing on the computer.

Ty doesn't look at me when he says, "She needs your passport."

I pull it from my bag and hand it to the woman who continues punching keys.

"We'll be lucky if we make the boarding," Ty says in a clipped voice.

"I'm sorry," I say.

"Are you?" he says, his voice low, and I hear the accusation underscoring the question.

The woman looks up and then quickly back at her computer screen. I feel my face heat up. I press my lips together and don't answer.

We don't speak again until the plane is in the air.

The seats are in business class, but I can tell that Ty finds them less than satisfactory based on the way he glances toward the first-class cabin, as if that's where he belongs.

"Did you speak with anyone else after we talked?" I finally ask.

"No," he says abruptly. "I did check her credit card usage. There have been no charges since the bar Peyton said they went to."

My stomach drops with this information. Kylie constantly uses her credit card. Starbucks a couple of times a day. Amazon. The mall.

"Where could she be?" I ask, my voice breaking on the words.

"I don't know," he says in a tone that I do not recognize as the Ty of recent years. Confident. Arrogant. This is the Ty from long, long ago. A version of him that I'm not sure I even remembered once existed.

"What if we don't find her?" he says.

"Don't," I say. "Please. Don't say that."

He stares at the seat in front of him for a minute or more before he looks over at me and says, "How did we get here, Lizzy?"

I let myself meet his gaze and see in his eyes someone I once knew. "One choice at a time," I say.

"And you think I'm responsible for all the choices that got us here?"

"No," I say. "It takes two people to mess up a marriage."

"I know I'm more to blame than you are," he says, surprising me with the sincerity in the admission. "And both of us have plenty of reason to be mad at each other right now."

For emphasis, he runs the palm of his hand over his bruised jaw. Guilt stabs at me. I start to respond, but he stops me with, "When we get back to Virginia, Lizzy, we're going to need each other. We both need to be there for Kylie. Can we do that?"

I think of our daughter, and a dozen different scenarios of horror try to overtake my deliberate calm. I know that Ty is right. And that nothing else in the world matters right now except getting our daughter back. Making sure she is safe.

"We'll do whatever we need to do," Ty says, and I hear that some of his confidence has returned. His belief that if you push back hard enough, the world will give you what you want. "Okay?" he asks, reaching over to take my hand in his.

"Okay," I say, and force myself not to pull away.

45

Lizzy

I WANT TO SLEEP. I long for the oblivion it would bring. The blanking out of everything that is happening right now.

But I can't. And I know I won't. It feels as if every muscle in my body is strung tight with worry. The fearful kind that overtakes every cell, every thought.

As a mother, it's something I've thought of countless times. What if someone took my child?

When Kylie was a little girl, I was anxious about it to the point of overprotectiveness. In public places, the grocery store, restaurants, I wouldn't let her out of my sight.

Ty said I smothered her and that I needed to loosen the apron strings. As she grew older, I forced myself to be more reasonable about my fears, but it wasn't easy, and even after she became a teenager and started going out with friends, this was something I struggled with.

So I did everything I could think of to increase her ability to protect herself. Anything I could think of to encourage her to be careful.

I stare out the window of the plane at the clouds below, feeling numb with disbelief.

I think about how little we actually know and consider other explanations for where Kylie might be. Ty said she left the bar with the singer from the band.

The irony of this does not escape me. Instead, it pries the lid from the guilt waiting to get a foothold alongside the worry. Maybe Kylie is with him. It's not outside the realm of possibility. The past week of my own life is evidence enough of that.

But why wouldn't she be answering her phone? Why would she not tell Peyton where she was going?

I don't think she would do that. Even if she completely lost her head over a boy. She would let someone know where she was.

This reality pushes hard against my heart, and I feel the bruise starting to form.

Would this have happened if I hadn't gone ahead and taken the trip to Italy by myself?

Logically, I know these dots do not connect. But I also know I made a choice to step outside my regular role of wife and mother. I was somewhere I shouldn't have been. Doing something I never should have been doing.

Ty shifts in the seat beside me. He raises his head, looks at me with sleep-cloudy eyes. "You should try to get some rest."

"I'm okay."

"I keep thinking," he says, resting his head against the seat. "She wanted to come home this weekend. If I hadn't come to Italy to find you—"

He stops there and shuts his eyes. But he doesn't need to finish. I know what he was going to say. If he hadn't come to Italy to find me, none of this would ever have happened.

46

Ty

THE PLANE LANDS at Dulles almost exactly nine-and-a-half hours after leaving Rome. You feel like you haven't slept in a week and realize that you probably look like it, too.

You slept a couple of hours, at least. You're pretty sure Lizzy didn't sleep any.

As soon as the plane lands, you start trying to call Peyton but only get her voice mail. You dial the number the detective left for you, but get a message there as well.

You're among the first off the plane, and you lead the way down the corridor, checking the signs for baggage claim. After getting your luggage and forging your way through customs, you notice a group of photographers standing up ahead. You stop, and Lizzy bumps into you from behind.

"What is it?" she asks.

"There," you hear one of them say. "That's them."

Lizzy shakes her head. "They're not here for us, are they?"

But then suddenly, the photographers and what appear to be reporters with microphones, rush toward them, all speaking at once.

"Mr. and Mrs. Harper, could we have a word with you, please?"

A tall blonde woman in a pencil thin, navy dress steps out from the throng and says, "Mrs. Harper, we understand that you've been spending time in Italy with Ren Sawyer, the lead singer with Temporal."

"And Mr. Harper," another man behind her speaks up. "Is it true that you had an altercation with Mr. Sawyer while you were in Italy?"

You reach for Lizzy's hand and start pulling her through the pile of media people. Someone from the airport begins to shout at the reporters, telling them they need to back away from the corridor so that other passengers might exit.

You lead Lizzy through the crowd, both of you with your heads down, even as you feel the flash of light and sound of cameras clicking away.

"Is it true, Mr. Harper, that your daughter is missing, or was that just a ploy to get your wife away from Ren Sawyer?"

You start to stop and give the reporter the swing he deserves. But now it's Lizzy pulling you, past the airport gates, walking faster and faster until finally, they are out of sight. Only then do you let go of her hand.

47

Lizzy

IT FEELS AS if the drive from D.C. to Charlottesville takes days, when, in actuality, it's only a couple of hours.

Ty drives the rental car at the speed limit and over when he can. About halfway there, he finally gets Kylie's roommate on the phone, only to learn that there's still no news, no sign of her anywhere.

"What do we do when we get there?" I ask, as soon as he finishes talking with Peyton. "How do we even know where to begin?"

"We'll start with the police," Ty says. "We'll just start there, and we won't stop until we find her."

I stare out the window at the green pastures we're passing, and I can't help but think of other parents I've seen interviewed on the news. Their optimism in the beginning. Their determination to bring their children home. And then later, down the road when they still haven't been found, those same parents, weary and beaten down, defeated.

I close my eyes and I start to pray. I know in my heart there is absolutely nothing else I can do.

48

Kylie

"WE'RE PROBABLY NOT going to get out of this, you know."

Erin's voice rouses Kylie from half-sleep. "Don't say that," she says.

"Well, you know it's most likely true."

"No, I don't."

They both get quiet, and Kylie begins trying to leaf through her memory for something, anything that might help them.

She thinks through the self-defense class her mom had made her take. Each of the tactics taught to her by a male instructor who insisted that if they knew the right things to do, it wouldn't matter how much stronger a man was. Smart trumped strength every time.

Except, Kylie realizes now, when the element of surprise is involved.

It's only then that she remembers the documentary she and her mom had watched together the year before Kylie left for college.

She hadn't wanted to watch it. She'd had plans to go out that night, and the last thing she'd wanted to do was stay home with her mom and watch TV. But her mom had already watched it, and she'd thought it was the kind of thing young girls could benefit from seeing.

It was about some teenage girl in California who had been abducted from her home by a man who took her to his house, and for the first couple of days, repeatedly raped her and told her he was going to kill her.

The point of the documentary was that for whatever reason, the girl felt that the best thing she could do was try and be a friend to her captor. Hope that he wouldn't see her as an object but as another human being.

So she forced herself to talk to him. Ask him questions about himself. Tell him things about herself. Personal things that she sensed they would have in common.

In doing this, she eventually gained his trust and was able to get away.

Kylie remembers sitting on the couch with her mom, watching the story unfold. Remembers how resentful and defiant she had been. Regret swoops through her for the way she'd spoken to her mom, for how she'd belittled the thought that there was anything to be gained from her staying home and watching the show.

She thinks then about the two men who had kidnapped her, the one who had said he didn't see anything wrong with sampling the goods.

And from there, Kylie begins to come up with a plan.

49

Ren

SOPHIA AND I wander around the villa for the first few hours after we get back from the airport.

I finally settle into a chair outside by the pool, a book on my lap. The words refuse to process though, and I close it, dropping my head back to stare at the blue sky above.

The house feels completely empty now. The only thing I can compare Lizzy's leaving to is losing my brother. Knowing I would not see him again in this life. Watching Lizzy walk away from the car at the airport felt final in the same way.

It hardly makes sense, given how little time we actually spent together. But the connection I feel with her is one I've never known with any other woman. And I've known a lot of women.

The difference with Lizzy is that she knows next to nothing about the life I've lived in the spotlight. When she looks at me, I think she sees the me before all of that, without all of that. And yet, I'm not diminished in her eyes.

As for her reaction to the truth about my brother's death, I had expected her to look at me completely different. To see me as I see myself.

But that hadn't been the case.

I could see that she felt compassion for me. But not blame. Only the quiet insistence that I eventually needed to forgive myself.

I want to.

I want to go on with life.

That much I do know now.

I look down at the puppy snuggled in the curve of my arm. I think of what a small thing it was to offer her safety and a home. A small thing for me, but a big thing for her. Doing that for her has given me a satisfaction I haven't felt in a very long time. And I realize that I want my life to be more of that kind of thing and less of what it has been for the past dozen years. If I'm going to stay on this earth, I'd like to work at changing things for others, making lives better in whatever way I can.

I have more money than I will ever be able to spend on myself. Money that can do a lot of good. I realize that continuing my career in any way will only mean something to me if I use it as a catalyst for good. And somewhere, deep in my heart, I think Colby would agree.

50

Lizzy

WE MEET WITH the police for several hours. I never imagined how many questions they could come up with to ask. They want to know everything. Her habits. Her friends. Any trouble she might ever have been in. Whether she's promiscuous. Does drugs. Drinks alcohol.

Detective Haley, the woman who asks most of the questions finally appears to take pity on us. She runs a hand through her thick auburn hair and says, "I think that's everything for now. I apologize for the intrusive nature of the questioning, but sometimes it's the smallest detail that helps us find a missing person."

"We understand," Ty says, his voice clipped in the way it gets when he wants to be done with a conversation.

The detective's phone rings. She picks it up. "Detective Haley."

We wait while she listens and finally says, "Okay. Thanks for letting me know."

"That was Detective Miller with the police department in Alexandria, Virginia," she says, putting down the phone and looking across the table at us. "They located the singer from the band. He's been questioned thoroughly. It sounds as if she did leave the room sometime during the night. He passed a lie detector test."

I absorb her words, at first relieved to know that he didn't have anything to do with her disappearance and then almost instantly sick with fear for all the other possible explanations. I lace my hands together in my lap, searching for the courage to ask my next question. "Will you find her?"

The detective looks at me with compassion in her eyes. I wonder how many other families she's had ask her this same question. "We're doing everything we can," she says. "Please. Know that we understand every hour counts. Your daughter's case has my full attention."

"Are you a mother?" I ask, my voice breaking across the word.

"Yes, I am."

We hold each other's gaze, and I see that she knows the place I'm in.

Ty stands abruptly, sliding his chair back, the legs making an awful screech against the tile floor. He reaches for my arm and pulls me to my feet. "Call us if you have anything," he says. "Anything at all."

And we leave the room.

WE WALK DOWN the hallway, silent all the way to the rental car. Once we're inside, we sit, staring out the windshield while cars pull in and out of the parking lot around us.

"I can't believe this has happened," I say, my voice barely audible. "What if they don't find her, Ty? What if we never see her again?"

He shifts in his seat, reaches out and pulls me to him. I press my face against his shirt, and the tears gush up and out of me. My sobs are painful, wrenching from my chest with volcanic force. I cry until I have nothing left inside me. I'm limp with grief, and in contrast, Ty holds himself stiff as if it's up to him to keep me from completely dissolving altogether.

"You can't think like that, Lizzy," he finally says, rubbing the back of my hair with the palm of his hand. "We have to stay strong for her."

"I don't know if I can," I say. "The waiting. It's horrible."

"I know. But let's think of it as every minute that passes is a minute that brings us closer to seeing her again."

"Will we?"

"See her again?"

I nod, mute. "Yes," he says. "Yes."

And I hang onto that. Like it's the strongest limb on the strongest tree standing right in the tornado's path.

51

Ren

SOMETHING HITS ME in the face, and I come awake from a dead sleep.

I sit straight up in bed, forcing my eyes open.

Sophia starts barking from the pillow next to mine. I reach for her, telling her to hush, only then realizing someone is in the room.

Gretchen stands a few feet away, holding a newspaper in her hand, fury altering her normally placid expression.

"Did you just hit me with that?" I ask, rubbing my jaw. And then, awareness settling in, "What are you doing here, Gretchen?"

"Good question," she says. "If I had an ounce of common sense, I'd put myself on the opposite end of the globe from you."

I run a hand through the back of my hair, and say, "You're most likely right about that."

"You ass!" she screams, throwing the whole newspaper at me now. "How could you, Ren?"

I pick up the paper, see myself in a photo with Lizzy. We're kissing in San Gimignano, the sun setting just behind us. I feel a stab of longing in the pit of my stomach, longing for Lizzy. I miss her so much I have to close my eyes against the wave of pain.

"I wanted to come here with you. And you said no. You wanted to be alone. Right! Did you have her planned all along, Ren?"

"Gretchen, no—"

"No? Who the hell is she anyway? Some housewife from Virginia? That's my competition?" She starts to laugh then, and I realize she's been drinking.

"Hey," I say. "Why don't you get a shower and some sleep and then we'll talk?"

"Oh, sure," she says, waving a hand in the air and stumbling backward in her heels. "As long as you can put me off, you're fine. Right, Ren? Well, you're not putting me off anymore. I'm a model! A supermodel! I have fans! Guys hit on me all the time."

"Gretchen—"

"What does she have? How did she get you? It doesn't even make sense! How could you do this to me? I'm so humiliated, Ren!" As if her knees have given way beneath her, she sinks to the floor and buries her face in her hands, sobbing.

I get out of bed and walk over to her, dropping down beside her. I put a hand on her shoulder, but she jerks away.

"Don't you dare touch me," she says.

"I never meant to hurt you," I say.

"Does it matter whether you meant to or not?" she says, looking up at me with tears streaming down her cheeks.

"No, I don't guess it does. But I'm sorry for it."

She stares at me for several long seconds and then reaches out to cup the side of my face with her hand. "Can we fix this?" she asks softly.

I don't want to say it, but I know I owe her the truth. I shake my head. "You didn't break it. I did. You deserve better treatment than what I've given you. I'm really sorry, Gretchen."

Her tears increase, and I hate myself for hurting her like this.

She gets to her feet, walks into the bathroom and closes the door behind her. In a few seconds, I hear the shower start.

52

Kylie

IT HAS BEEN a very long time since Kylie prayed.

But from the moment the idea comes to her, she doesn't stop praying that the next time one of the men comes into the room to check on them, it will be the one she needs it to be.

At least a couple of hours pass before she hears the door lock slide open, and a man steps inside the room. "Do you think I could ask you a favor?" she says.

"Probably not," the man says.

Recognizing his voice, she breathes a sigh of relief along with a silent thank you for the answer to her prayer.

Kylie forces herself to look directly at his face, manages a small smile when she says, "Is there any way I could possibly take a shower?" She waves a hand at the bottom of her dress. "I'm kind of a mess. It would be really nice to clean up a bit."

"No," he says, shaking his head. "I can't let you do that."

"I don't want to get you in trouble with your friend," Kylie says, "but I'm kind of miserable."

He frowns, considering her words before saying, "Well, it's not like he's in charge or anything."

"I mean . . . you could watch if you're afraid I might do something." Kylie holds her gaze steady against his. More than anything, she wants to reel away in disgust, but she keeps her expression compliant and waits for his answer, not wanting to appear too pushy.

He glances at his watch and looks as if he's struggling with an answer. "There's a bathroom down the hall. I guess if I go with you, it can't hurt anything. I imagine where you're going, they'll prefer you clean anyway."

"I prefer me clean," Kylie says. "Thank you."

He crosses the floor, leans over and inserts the key into the cuff attached to the bed. He puts it on her right wrist, locking her hands together.

Erin, quiet until now, says, "Please don't leave me here alone."

"I'll be back," Kylie says.

Outside in the hallway, he closes the door behind him and locks it with a key. "This way," he says, waving her left.

She follows him to a door at the end of the hall. He opens it, and then waits for her to step inside.

The bathroom is small, a sink, a toilet, a shower.

He closes the door behind them, looks at her and raises his hands in the air. "Well, hurry up if you're going to do it."

"Okay," she says. Her heart is pounding so hard, she can feel it in her throat. She holds up her handcuffed wrists and says, "I'll be a lot more effective without these."

He looks at her as if trying to decide what exactly she means. She forces her mouth to smile. "Or so I've been told," she says.

He doesn't take his eyes from hers as he reaches in his pocket and pulls out a key chain. He inserts the key in the lock one wrist at a time and removes the cuffs. "That should do it," he says with a half-grin on his mouth.

She reaches around to unzip the back of her dress, turning so that she can close her eyes as she lowers first one side and then the other. She tells herself she has no other choice. "Could you unhook my bra?" she asks.

She feels his fumbling fingers at the clasp, her skin rebelling to the touch. She slips out of it, dropping her dress with it. Her panties are last, and she hears his quick intake of breath as she slides them down.

He reaches around her and turns the shower on, the water spurting hard once and then falling in a steady stream. His arm brushes her breast as he pulls back, and she doesn't know if it's intentional or not, but she feels him tense.

She has no idea whether she can go through with this. She steps into the shower, letting the spray pummel her face and soak her hair. She feels him watching her. She makes herself look at him, as if inviting him in. She can see him breathing hard.

"Want to join me?" she asks, not even recognizing her own voice.

She glances at his pants for confirmation of exactly how much he would like to say yes. He's unbuttoning his shirt and starting on his zipper when a scream breaks through the door.

The sound is like a knife cutting through the air, a death scream, like someone's life is ending.

The man yanks up his zipper and roars at her, "You stay put!"

"Okay," she says.

He jerks out of the bathroom, slamming the door behind him. She hears a key in the lock.

There's a very small window across from the toilet. She knows they're on the second floor of the house because she'd heard the men coming up the stairs. She stretches on tiptoe to look out the window, but she can't see how far down it is.

It doesn't matter though. She knows this is her only hope. She glances at the door and sees a slide lock at the top. She slips it into place so that it is locked from inside as well.

She looks around for something to break the glass. A plunger stands just behind the toilet. She picks it up and holds the bottom with both hands, and then slams the wooden end into the window.

The first time, it doesn't break, and she feels the jarring in her elbows and shoulders.

She tries again, and this time the glass shatters. She punches as much of it out as she can.

Footsteps sound in the hall, and she knows she only has

seconds. He's coming back. She struggles into the opening, sticking her head through, first one shoulder and then another, praying the rest of her body will fit.

Now that she can see outside, she realizes the ground is two very high floors beneath her. A large boxwood sits just to the left of the window.

She wriggles her way through the opening until she is all but hanging by her feet. If only she could turn around and drop feet first, but there's no way to do it.

She hears him shoving against the door now, cursing the lock on the inside. She's so scared she can barely breathe. She can't do it. Can't make herself let go.

She hears the splintering of the wood as the door starts to give beneath his pounding shoulder. Within seconds, he'll be inside.

No choice.

She makes herself let go.

She falls.

53

Ty

YOU WONDER HOW you ever considered Winn a friend.

She'd arrived at the hotel a couple of hours ago, instantly establishing herself as protector over Lizzy. She refused to even meet your eyes, barely speaking at all. She'd led Lizzy inside the room that adjoins yours, all but closing the door in your face.

You stew in your own room for a bit, and then send her a text.

Meet me at the ice machine on this floor. Now.

You wait at the end of the hall a full five minutes before she finally shows up, ice bucket in one hand.

"What do you want, Ty?" she asks, sticking the bucket inside the machine and pushing the button.

"I want you to stay out of my marriage, Winn."

She turns around and glares up at you. "I'm here for Lizzy, Ty. In whatever capacity she needs me."

"I'm the one she needs here. She doesn't need you filling her head with stuff that doesn't matter now."

"Well, that's convenient, isn't it? Kylie disappears and your infidelity gets a pass?"

"That's beneath even you, Winn."

She actually looks ashamed for a moment before saying, "I never wanted to be put in the position of discovering your fling, Ty. But you know my loyalty is to Lizzy. And she deserves way better than what you were doing to her."

"Do you even know what she was doing in Italy with that—

"I saw what some paparazzi reporters said. Do I believe Lizzy would have been unfaithful to you first? No. I don't believe that for a second."

She picks up the ice bucket and walks down the hallway, back to Lizzy's room.

You want to go after her, yell at her to mind her own damn business. But you stay where you are. Silent. Because the truth is, she's right.

54

Ren

IT'S SIX IN the morning here. Midnight there. I know I shouldn't call her yet, but I can't stop myself.

I dial the number and wait in silence for a few moments, and then the ring.

Her voice, when she answers, is low and tired-sounding.

"I'm sorry for waking you," I say.

"You didn't," she answers.

"Hey," I say.

"Hey."

"How are you?"

"Not so good just now."

"No word yet?"

"No."

She sounds defeated and grief-stricken, and I wish I could find something to say that would erase both from her voice. Something to give her hope. "What can I do for you?" I ask.

"Nothing," she says softly. "I just want her back so badly."

"Can I come there? Just to be with you while you wait?"

A long pause follows my question. And I know I shouldn't have asked it. "Ren. My life has completely fallen apart. Some of it is my fault. I've got to do what I can to put it back together again."

"You're not being fair to yourself."

"Somehow, in the scheme of things, that doesn't seem so important right now."

"Lizzy, I miss you—"

"Ren. Please. We can't be. We. Can't. Be."

"Are you trying to convince me or yourself?" I say, hearing the frustration in my voice.

"You know it's true."

"No. I don't."

She sighs, and after a few seconds, says, "Even before this happened, we knew it. Two different worlds. We live in two different worlds."

"I want us to live in the same world."

"We don't always get what we want," she says, and I hear the resignation in her words.

"Lizzy—"

"I have to go. Good-bye, Ren."

I sit for a long time after she hangs up, Sophia climbing onto my lap. I rub her soft head while I wish I knew how to make myself let Lizzy go. That's what she's asked me to do. It's all she's asked me for. Why then does it feel so impossible?

55

Lizzy

FROM THE BED next to mine, Winn rises up on one elbow and squints at me through sleep-heavy eyes. "Was that who I think it was?"

I sit up with a pillow behind me and nod.

"Oh, my word. Ren Sawyer just called you on the telephone."

I don't answer because I don't know what I can say that won't remind me of how far I've mentally strayed from my marriage, my family.

"You don't need to feel guilty with me, Lizzy."

"I feel guilty, period."

"You didn't cause any of this."

I pick up a pillow and fold my arms around it, clutching it to my chest. "What if we don't find her?"

Winn gets out of her bed and slides into mine, putting her arm around my shoulder and cradling me the way I've seen her do with her children when something has gone wrong for them. "We will find her. We need to keep our faith in that. And you need to give yourself a break."

I press my face into the pillow, sobs rising up from deep inside me. Winn wraps both arms around me then, smoothing a hand across my hair.

"What's happened with Kylie has nothing to do with you going to Italy or meeting Ren Sawyer. The timing is nothing but coincidental. And if Ty had gone with you instead of staying here and bringing another woman into your bedroom, you never would have met Ren. Or at least not in the same way. Are you going to deny that?"

"Does it matter?"

"It matters. Ty's perfectly willing to let your judgment be clouded by guilt. I, on the other hand, am not."

"I just want her back," I say, fresh tears staining the pillowcase.

"Shh," she says. "I know. Just hold on, okay. Just hold on."

56

Kylie

SHE HAS NO idea which direction to take, but she starts running. Completely naked. Running. Feet pounding. Arms pumping. Running as if life will end if she stops. As she knows it very likely will.

She can't tell if he is behind her. If he will jump in a vehicle and tear off after her, overtaking her, running her down even.

She won't look back. Looking back will allow the fear to swallow her, pulling her beneath the surface like a drowning victim in the last moments of resistance. She veers off the narrow paved road and runs into the woods, knowing that at least here, he'll have to follow her on foot.

Her chest can barely pull in the air needed to keep oxygen flowing to her limbs. She steps on rocks that cut into her feet, but the pain is nothing compared to the fear.

The woods begin to thin, fade from trees to grass pasture. She keeps running, stride after stride, until she can feel her legs begin to fail her. She won't last much longer. No more energy. No more air.

And that's when she sees the house.

57

Lizzy

BY THE END of the day, I'm not sure I can make it through another one like this. Ty and Winn are at each other's throats. And while I know Winn is only standing up for me, I just want out of the conflict. I long for a quiet place where I can sit and wait for the phone to ring with news of Kylie.

My nerve endings feel as if they've been dipped in Tabasco sauce. I have to get out of the room for a while. "I'm going to take a walk," I say to Winn. "I'll be back in a bit."

"I can go with you," she says.

"That's okay," I say. "I think I need to clear my head."

Ty gives me a disapproving look, but says nothing.

Winn says, "Don't forget your phone."

I grab it from the nightstand and walk out the door.

I take the stairs and let myself out a side entrance. The late spring afternoon is warm, and I welcome the feel of the air on my skin in comparison to the freezing air conditioner of our room.

The hotel connects to a park. I find the entrance and start to run, even though I'd intended to walk. The exertion feels good. I push myself, faster, faster until I can barely draw in breath. When I stop, I lean over with my palms on my knees, sucking in oxygen.

I walk to a nearby bench and sink onto the wood seat, sliding down and letting my head rest against the back. I have no idea how to exist in this place we're in. This waiting place. There's only been one experience in my life I can compare it to. When Kylie was a little girl, we had a scare over some blood work that came back indicating she might have leukemia. During the second round of testing while the doctors determined whether she had it or not, all I could do was push myself through every phase of the day. Functioning like a robot that can only do what it has been programmed to do.

I have never known the kind of relief I knew the day we got the news that Kylie did not have the disease. For a long time after the nurse who had called me hung up the phone, I sat on my kitchen barstool, staring out the window, letting my gratitude fill every pore in my body. I could not bear the thought of losing her, and to be given that reprieve was the greatest blessing of my life.

And now here I am, asking to be blessed yet again in the same way. Tragic events befall countless people every single day on this earth. Why should I think I should be spared?

I don't have an answer for that. My needs are not more worthy than the next person praying for a miracle. And I know that's exactly what I'm asking for. I drop my head. I pray again, from the bottom of my soul, for my daughter's safety.

58

Lizzy

I SEE THE police car at the front of the hotel as I round the corner to exit the park.

The lights on top are spinning, throwing out alarming crisscrosses. My heart thumps hard in my chest, and I feel suddenly sick with apprehension. I run as fast as I can toward the car, forcing myself not to process the scenarios pounding through my brain.

A police officer steps out of the hotel just as I get to the main door. "Are you here about my daughter?" I ask, breathless.

"Mrs. Harper?"

"Yes," I manage, barely able to get the word out.

"Can you come with me, please?"

"What is it?" I ask, panic welling up.

Just then Ty and Winn come running out of the hotel. "They're taking us to the police station," Ty says.

"What's happened?" I ask, and I'm pleading now. I don't think I can stand another second of not knowing.

The three of us slide into the back of the car, the officer getting behind the wheel. He turns on the siren and pulls quickly out of the parking lot and onto the highway.

I look at Ty, feeling the tears running down my face. "Can he not tell us anything?" I ask.

"He said he was only asked to pick us up and take us to the station. He doesn't know anything else."

Winn slides her arm around my shoulders and pulls me up against her. "Shh, Lizzy. We have to assume the best. Okay? Don't let yourself consider anything else."

But I can't help it. I am tortured by fear of what we are about to learn. I put my face in my hands and try not to sob out loud, my shoulders shaking with silent force.

The drive takes almost fifteen minutes. The cruiser swings into the lot of a building marked Charlottesville Police. As soon as the car stops, Ty opens the door and Winn and I slide across the seat to get out.

"This way, please," the officer says, waving for us to follow him.

We walk quickly inside the building, our footsteps echoing on the hard floor of a long, well-lit hallway. At the very end, the officer knocks on a door, sticks his head inside and then waves for us to step in.

In the corner of the room sits Kylie. Huddled inside a blanket, her face pale and drawn. She looks up and spots us, instantly dissolving into tears. Ty and I both go to her, dropping onto our knees and enfolding her in our mutual embrace. All three of us are crying then. I feel Winn's hand on my shoulder.

"I'm so sorry," Kylie says, on a broken sob. "I'm so very sorry."

"Thank God," I say. "You're okay. You're okay."

59

Ren

I DO A GOOGLE search for "Kylie Harper" as soon as I get out of bed.

The first result is the *Huffington Post* with **Missing UVa Student Found.**

I click on the link and wait for the article to come up, and then quickly skim it.

Kylie Elizabeth Harper, 20, was found alive late yesterday after she had been missing for five days.

Harper was apparently abducted in Charlottesville, Virginia on her way back to her dorm after seeing a band in the college town. One source says she managed to escape through a second-floor window of the house where she was being held.

Investigators say Harper claims there was another girl being held in the house with her, and, that after she escaped, the kidnappers took the other girl and disappeared. There are still no reports of the second girl's whereabouts.

I glance at the beginning of the article again, reread the first line with an incredible sense of relief. For her. For Lizzy. And a sick feeling for the other girl involved.

I pick up my phone and type in a text message.

So relieved for you and your family. If you need me for anything, I'm here for you.

I want to say more. But force myself to put the phone down and leave it at that.

60

Ty

YOU TRY TO make things like they once were. Back when Kylie was a little girl, and you came home from work at dinner time. Back when you all ate at the table together. When you didn't use work as an escape from a life you'd begun to grow bored with.

Kylie decides not to finish the semester at UVa. The first two weeks after she moves home, you don't leave for the office until the three of you have coffee together, heading out only after you've all talked about what you're doing for the day and interesting stuff in the newspaper. It's all very normal. Very family like.

Then you ask yourself why it feels like you're all trying too hard. Acting out roles instead of just being yourselves in a way that feels comfortable and right.

As for your life at the office, you're all business. No more affairs. You're committed to doing right by Lizzy. There's been no mention of that rock star loser, and so you're willing to pretend that it never happened.

And if you try hard enough to act normal, be normal, then there's no reason life can't go back to what it once was. You're willing to make sacrifices for it. Convinced that in the end, it will be worth it. Because, after all, human nature is such that it's not until you nearly lose something that you realize what you have.

61

Kylie

KYLIE KNOWS THAT she has to start getting out of the house.

But she can't seem to make herself.

She's closed herself in, sealed out the world beyond her front door, as if in doing so, she won't have to think about the ugly stuff she hadn't really believed existed before her abduction.

It was all stuff she heard on the news, things that happened to other people, other families.

She dreams about it nearly every night. Wakes up in a sweat, gasping for air. And she sees the other girl's face—Erin's face—hears her voice. Constantly wonders what those men did with her.

She still hasn't been found. Kylie has begun to think they will never find her.

Her guilt is mind-numbing, choking. It sits like a concrete

blanket on her shoulders, and it is all she can do to move through a complete day beneath its weight.

She's sitting on the screened porch one afternoon with her MacBook on her lap, staring out across the back yard when her mom comes out, handing her a glass of iced tea.

"Thought you might be thirsty," she says.

"Thanks," Kylie says, setting it on the table next to her.

"How are you doing?" her mom asks, a now familiar concern darkening her eyes.

"I'm okay. Try not to worry about me, Mom. I'll get there eventually."

"I know."

"I just can't stop thinking about Erin," Kylie says, anguish sharpening the edges of her voice. "If she hadn't screamed when she did, I never would have gotten away. I know she did it intentionally so I would have a chance. It probably cost her her life."

"And the first thing you did was run for help. There was nothing else you could do," she says, reaching out to squeeze Kylie's hand. "You were no match for those men."

Kylie considers this, knowing logically that her mom is right. But logic has little sway over guilt. And so she says nothing.

"You have a lot of healing to do, honey. And that's going to take however long it takes. You were a victim too."

"It's just . . . I can't stand to think of where she might be." The tears come in full force then, and Kylie can do nothing to stop them.

Her mom gets up, scoots onto the chair beside her and folds her close in a tight embrace. "Shh," she says. "I'm so sorry, honey. For everything you've been through. For everything you're feeling. If I could take it from you, I would."

"I know," Kylie says, burying her face in her mother's neck and crying until she has no more tears to cry. They sit, silent, while a neighbor's dog barks, a car drives by on the road in front of the house, and life goes on.

The ice in her tea has completely melted when Kylie finally speaks again. "Mom?"

"Hmm?"

"I came across a story on the Internet about you and Ren Sawyer in Italy together. Was that true?"

Kylie feels her mother stiffen, as if bracing herself against the conversation to come.

"Parts of it," she says softly.

"You really met him?" she asks.

"I didn't know who he was at first. I think we both really needed a friend just then for completely different reasons."

"Is that all you were? Friends?"

"In the end, yes," she says.

"Can you I ask you something?"

"Of course."

"If what happened to me had never happened, would you and Daddy still be together?"

She's silent for several long moments, before saying, "Part of me wants to gloss over our history, Kylie. Tell you, yes, absolutely. But another part of me feels that I owe you honesty. You're an adult now. You know that life gets complicated sometimes."

"I know that Daddy has cheated on you."

Her mom draws in a sharp breath, as if a knife has just been inserted in the center of her chest. "Kylie—"

"I never wanted to admit it," she says. "I guess I wanted to believe you were to blame because of what I read in your journal that time. But that wasn't right. Or fair to you. I'm sorry, Mom. For all the times I was so ugly to you. I'm sorry."

She kisses Kylie's hair and shakes her head. "Let's leave all that in the past, okay? I think we've both had a clear reminder of how precious life is. How uncertain and unpredictable. I don't want to take a minute of it for granted."

"Neither do I," Kylie says.

They sit quiet for a bit, comfortable with each other in a way they haven't been for a very long time.

"I was thinking I might take a drive on the Blue Ridge Parkway this afternoon," her mom finally says, "and bring my camera along. Would you like to go?"

"I would," Kylie says. "I really would."

62

Lizzy

THREE MONTHS PASS in a blink.

I watch Kylie for signs of healing and begin to see a little progress each day. She's begun to show an interest in photography, and we go shopping one afternoon to buy her a camera. It's something we're doing together, and I love that we can share it. Comparing shots, talking about places we might like to go, that we would love to capture with our cameras. I don't think I'm biased in saying she has an eye for angles, for unique takes. There's something about the camera being between her and the world that is allowing her to ease back into it. To begin seeing life as beautiful once again, the harsh, ugly edges of her experience fading for bits of time here and there, anyway.

As for me and life outside anything that doesn't relate to Kylie, I simply don't let myself think about it. My commitment to Kylie is complete, my needs secondary at best. I've had a few texts from Ren, but I've deleted them without reading them. It seems better not to let his words into my head, my heart. Because I have chosen to make this life with Ty, with Kylie, what is important to me.

I have to give Ty credit. I've never seen him try so hard. He calls me throughout the day. Sends me flowers. Plans weekend escapes for the three of us.

It's nearly ideal. As perfect as I had once imagined our life could be, if Ty were able to refocus some of his career ambition to a home life with us. And that's what he's done.

So I try. Tell myself I will see him through new eyes. Truly forgive the past.

I've been given a second chance with my daughter. I'm reminded of the enormity of this gift on a daily basis. Even more so because of the fact that Kylie and I have found common ground and our love for each other means everything to me.

For that, I can wipe the slate clean. Start from our new beginning. Block my mind of any what-ifs that try to rise up with Ren's name attached to them.

What kind of mother would I be if I did anything other than that?

63

Kylie

KYLIE WAKES UP one morning to the knowledge that it's time she leaves the house, alone. She's at the kitchen table, reading a book on her Kindle and finishing a pot of coffee when she looks across the table at her mom and says, "I think I'll go into the city and take Dad to lunch today."

Her mom glances up in surprise. "Want me to go with you?"

"That's okay. I kind of think I need to venture out on my own."

"Are you sure you're ready?"

"Yeah. I think so."

"Do you want to let him know you're coming?"

"I think I'll surprise him."

"I'm sure he'll be happy to see you."

She helps clean up the kitchen and then goes upstairs to shower, irrational apprehension gnawing at her with the thought of driving alone to the city, parking in the dimly lit parking garage next to her dad's office building. She could give in to it. Wait another day. But it isn't going to get any easier. In fact, she is pretty sure that every day she lets fear get the better of her, the more difficult it will ever be to conquer it.

Her mom watches from the front door as she backs out of the driveway and waves reassuringly, as if she has the whole thing completely under control.

She drives the fifteen miles or so with a white-knuckle grip on the steering wheel, blasting Spotify tracks through the car's Bluetooth to distract her from anything other than watching the miles slide by on her odometer.

She hits the Interstate that leads to downtown, and then takes the exit that lets her off a few streets up from the parking garage. She drives straight to it, turns in and gets her ticket, taking the first available spot. She gets out of the car quickly, hits the remote lock and runs to the elevator, as if she is late for an appointment instead of being terrified by ghosts she cannot see.

Her dad's office is on the seventh floor. She gets off the elevator and speaks to the receptionist, the same red-haired grandmother who has occupied the position since Kylie was a little girl. Her name is Edith, and she gets up from her seat to walk around the desk and give Kylie a hug. She doesn't need to say anything about what happened to her. Her embrace says it all, and Kylie returns her hug with gratitude.

When Kylie steps back, she manages a wobbly smile and

says, "I thought I'd surprise my dad and take him out to lunch."

"Well, I know that will make his day. You go on back, honey. And take good care of yourself, okay?"

"I will, Edith. Thank you."

Kylie doesn't allow her gaze to stray to the open doors of the offices along the hallway leading to her dad's office. She's not sure she can handle another encounter just now, and she hurries to the end of the hall. The door is half-open, and she slightly pushes on it and sticks her head inside.

Her dad is standing in front of the window that runs the width of the office. A woman has her arms around his neck, and they are kissing like two people who cannot get enough of each other.

The sound that escapes Kylie's throat isn't intentional. In fact, if she could have stepped back out of the office, silent and unnoticed, that is exactly what she would have chosen to do.

But her dad looks up just then, spots her and releases a heavy sigh. "Kylie," he begins.

She doesn't wait, though, to hear what he has to say. What is there to say? That one picture tells her everything she needs to know.

64

Lizzy

KYLIE ARRIVES HOME far sooner than I expected her back, the streaks on her face clear evidence that she's been crying.

I lead her to the living room couch where we both sit for a long time without speaking.

"He's a liar," Kylie finally says, her voice muffled against my shoulder.

"Who?" I ask, but somehow, I think I already know.

"Daddy. I walked in on him and some woman in his office."

She doesn't add more. But she doesn't need to. I wait for the stab of hurt the words should induce, but I think deep down, I've known it was just a matter of time.

I pull her tighter against me and say, "It's okay, Kylie. Thank you for telling me."

"But he's been lying to you. Acting as if everything was good again."

"I think maybe he wanted it to be."

"Are you defending him?" she asks, her voice rising.

"Of course not. But the two of us don't make each other happy anymore. So maybe this is the reminder I needed that a marriage should be so good that the desire to stray from it never occurs to either person."

"Is there such a thing anymore?" Kylie asks, clearly disbelieving.

"I have to believe so. Yes."

"He has no right to hurt you this way."

"I won't lie and say it doesn't hurt. It does. But probably not for the right reasons. We're going to be okay, you and me. It might take a little time, but we're going to be all right. Deal?"

Kylie nods against my shoulder. "Deal."

65

Lizzy

IT DOESN'T HAPPEN overnight, but my promise to Kylie does come true.

Life can change tremendously over the course of a year, and ours does.

Kylie has gone back to school, determined to finish her degree. I know the fears are still there, but with therapy and pure will on her part, she manages to mostly keep them at bay.

She's no longer my little girl, or my sullen teenager, or my standoffish college student. She is grown-up now, tarnished by some of the disillusionment that comes with being an adult, but her shine is still there, and I love the relationship we now have with each other. Our conversations never end. Texting allows us to talk nonstop throughout the day, even when she's in class or I'm working on my photography. And we talk every night before bedtime.

I cannot deny that good does come from bad sometimes, even though none of us would wish to experience it.

I'm out to dinner one night with Winn, sharing these thoughts with her when she says, "Don't you think it's time for you to move on, Lizzy?"

"I have moved on," I say.

"Ty has remarried," she reminds me. "And you haven't even been out on a date."

"I'm hardly interested in basing what I do on what Ty is doing."

"Nor should you be. But you deserve to be happy. To have someone good in your life."

"I have plenty of good in my life. A daughter who loves me. A best friend who indulges my need for an occasional fine meal and talks about good books with me. What else do I need?"

"A man," she says bluntly. "Have you even tried to get in touch with him?"

I don't need to ask who she's talking about. "No. I haven't, and I'm not going to."

"Because you're a chicken," she says.

"I'm not a chicken. Whatever happened between us, or what might have happened between us, was just a blip in time, that's all."

"A blip during that time. That doesn't mean it can't have another time. Like now."

"Winn. There are some things you learn to leave alone.

Thinking I could have something with a man like Ren . . . that I need to leave alone."

"But what if he wanted to see you? Would you turn him down?"

"That's not going to happen. He's gone on with his life. I read somewhere that he's no longer performing but developing new talent, starting up other bands."

"Is that a career that excludes having love in his life?"

I roll my eyes. "I didn't say I'd read that he'd become a monk. To the contrary, I'm sure."

"You never answered my question."

"What?"

"Would you see him if he wanted to see you?"

"He doesn't," I say. "Now, can we get back to our bottle of wine?"

66

Ren

THERE IS NO doubt in my mind that I am taking a risk.

Possibly one where I will make a fool of myself and end up regretting that I ever climbed out on this particular limb.

At the same time, I'm pretty sure I will regret not trying.

I stand in front of the hotel-room dressing mirror, making a last-minute adjustment to my tie. I don't remember the last time I wore one, and I second-guess whether I should just go with the shirt and jacket.

But Lizzy's friend, Winn, had said suits would be the norm. And I have no desire to stand out among Lizzy's peers as a stereotypical rock star in torn blue jeans and a T-shirt.

I wonder, not for the first time, if I should let her know I'm coming. Do I owe her that? Is this too far out in left field?

I force myself to put aside the questions, leave on the tie and head for the elevator.

There is only one way to find out if I have made more of

what Lizzy and I shared in Italy than it really was. Time and imagination can do that. Seeing her face to face is how I will get my answer. And if I'm honest, I'm afraid if I call her, she'll tell me not to come.

So I go with the element of surprise. It's the only card I have left to play.

67

Lizzy

IT'S ONE OF those things you dream about but never think will really happen.

I stand in the middle of the room, taking in the framed photographs on the surrounding walls, and even though they're mine, I can't help but admire them. Feel proud of them, like children I have raised to a respectable degree of success.

The gallery is crowded. Mine isn't the only work being shown tonight. Three other photographers have displays in adjoining rooms. It feels really nice to be a part of it, to achieve recognition not for the sake of recognition, but for validation of something I love to do and might possibly be able to make a living at.

"Clearly, you know San Gimignano."

Recognition instantly washes over me. I can't move, can't make myself turn around because I don't want to be wrong.

But he reaches out and turns me to face him. I'm not wrong. He really is here.

"Ren," I say, his name barely more than a whisper.

"Hey, Lizzy," he says, his gaze drinking in my face, dropping lower to take in my dress, my bare legs, my high heels.

"How did you . . . what are you?—"

"Winn called me about the show. I hope you don't mind that I came."

"No," I say, shaking my head. "I can't believe you're really here."

"I wasn't sure you would be okay with it."

Kylie walks up to stand beside me just then. I look at her, preparing to babble some explanation, but she smiles and sticks out her hand to Ren. "It's about time my mom let me meet you."

"You're Kylie," Ren says, shaking her hand and smiling the smile that would do to Kylie's insides exactly what it had done to mine the first time he turned it on me.

"It's awesome to meet you," she says, disbelief underlining each word.

"It's awesome to meet you," he says.

Winn slinks into sight then, her expression hopeful and a little wary. "Am I in the doghouse or not?" she asks, looking at me.

"You definitely should be," I say.

"I'll take that as a no," she says, with a look of relief.

Ren shoves his hands in his pockets and says, "So about that San Gimignano piece? I'm interested in that one."

I shake my head. "You don't have to do that."

"Oh, but I want to. You see I have some really good memories of that town."

"You do?" I say softly.

"I do. And with that photograph, every time I walk by it, I'll be reminded of those memories. I think that's a good thing. Do you?"

"I guess it could be," I allow, feeling Kylie and Winn staring at me as if they aren't sure who I am.

"Well, why don't we agree on a price, and then to celebrate, I'd like to take you three ladies out to dinner after the show."

"Is that your limo out front?" Kylie asks, reverting to teenage awe as her face lights up with excitement.

"We'll have plenty of room," he says. "And I've got champagne in the back. We can enjoy it without having to worry about driving."

"Wow," Kylie says, and then looking at me, "Are we going, Mom?"

"I'm not sure you're going to let me say no," I say, smiling.

"All right then," Ren says, taking my arm and leading me toward the San Gimignano photo. "Let's get business squared away." He leans in and says close to my ear, "And as long as you're in the mode of saying yes, I have another question or two for you. Later. When we're alone."

"Oh, you do?" I say, letting myself look into his eyes

without bothering to hide how happy I am to see him, how much I've missed him.

"Hold that thought," he says, brushing my cheek with his lips. "First things first. Now about the price you have on this spectacular photo. I don't think you're charging nearly enough."

I laugh. "But you're the customer. You shouldn't mind."

"I know what it's worth though, right?" he asks.

"Maybe," I concede.

"Then I should get to set the price. Right?"

"You're far too used to getting your way," I say.

"Where you're concerned," he says, leaning in to kiss me full on the mouth, before adding, "Let's hope the trend continues."

68

Lizzy

Eight Months Later

THE TREND CONTINUES.

How in the world can a woman say no to Ren Sawyer?
I certainly can't. Not when he asks me to finish our driving
tour of Italy. Six months venturing from one town to
another, stopping whenever we feel like it, eating our weight
in pasta and Tiramisu.

He buys a Range Rover so we have plenty of space this
time, Sophia napping on the back seat unless she chooses to sit
on my lap and look out the window at the vineyards flowing
by, hillside towns in the distance.

It feels like a dream, and there are times when I am
convinced it can be nothing else. I take thousands of pictures,

going through them at night and deleting the less spectacular ones, keeping the others.

While I'm taking pictures of everything in sight, Ren begins writing in a journal. He has an idea for a book about his experiences with his brother and their band. It seems like a sort of catharsis for him. I know he won't cut himself any slack in the picture he paints of his success as well as his regrets.

Putting the truth out for the world to not only see, but judge him by, is a form of restitution for him where his brother is concerned. At some point along the way, I realize that although he will never forgive himself for what he considers a betrayal of his brother, he is determined to live in a way that would make Colby proud.

And I am proud of him for his determination to face his past, accept it and his mistakes in a way that still allows him to find joy in life.

And that, I think I can say, we've both done.

I'm grateful for every day. Kylie's abduction has made me realize how very fragile our lives are. How quickly it all can change. How unimaginable our losses can be.

I have a relationship with my daughter now that means more to me than I can ever put into words. She's getting her masters degree in psychology and wants to work with victims traumatized by criminal acts committed against them. She's decided to work on her degree at Stanford in California, needing a change of scenery from Charlottesville and all the memories it holds for her.

I think it is a good decision. She's met someone, a South Carolina boy who looks at her as if she has all the answers to the universe. They both fly to Venice and meet us for a two-week stay, and I really can't imagine life getting any better than the warm days we spend winding through the treasure trove of Venetian streets, lazing along its canals on sleek gondolas, and eating the wonderful food available at every corner.

Then Ren asks me another question.

At the top of the Spanish steps in Rome. On a beautiful, cloudless June afternoon.

He's wearing sunglasses, but not the baseball cap he usually wears in public places. There are people all around us. "Are you sure we should be here?" I ask him. "You're likely to get mobbed."

He doesn't answer me, but takes my hand and moves to the step below me, dropping down on one knee.

My lips part in surprise and my heart starts beating a thousand miles an hour. "Ren. What are you—"

He reaches in his pocket and pulls out a small blue Tiffany box tied with a white ribbon. He hands it to me and says, "Will you open it, please?"

I take it from him, staring at the lid and then raising my gaze to his. "Ren, there are people looking—"

"Open it," he says again. "Please."

Around us, people are starting to aim phones in our direction, pictures snapping. I hear a girl's voice say, "Oh, my gosh, that's Ren Sawyer!"

"Ren—"

"Please, Lizzy."

And so I untie the white ribbon, lift the lid, pull out the inner box and slowly open it.

The diamond catches the sunlight, a work of art against its velvet background. I try to speak but I can't make a single word come out.

"Lizzy, will you marry me?" Ren asks. I lift my gaze to his again and see the uncertainty in his eyes, realizing suddenly that he's afraid I'll say no. Unbelievable as that is to me.

"Why here?" I ask, glancing around at the people smiling and staring at us.

"Because I want the world to know I love you. That I want to spend my life with you. That you're the woman I've been waiting for."

I feel the tears well in my eyes, slide down my cheeks. He reaches up and wipes them away with his thumb.

"Will you?" he repeats.

I nod once, laughing and crying at the same time. Cheers erupt around us.

Ren stands and slips his arms around my waist, pulling me to him. Church bells toll in the distance, taxi horns sound from below the Spanish steps. But it all fades away as he lowers his mouth to mine, kissing me in a way he's never kissed me before, as if I'm his, as if I always will be.

I kiss him back with awareness of this and then say it out loud. "Yes. Yes, I will marry you, Ren Sawyer."

And the trend continues.

That Month in Tuscany

69

Ren

Epilogue

THE SUN IS JUST coming up on the Mediterranean horizon. I can see it beginning its ascent to the sky through the glass door of our bedroom.

I've been awake for a while now, but it's not because I couldn't sleep. I just don't want to. I do this a lot. Wake up before she does so I can watch her sleeping. She usually opens her eyes pretty quickly, as if she can feel me looking at her.

This morning is no exception.

She comes awake slowly, blinking once and then bringing me into focus. "Good morning," she says, her voice husky in the way it is before she has her coffee.

"Morning," I say, reaching out to brush the back of my hand across her cheek.

She stares into my eyes and brushes her lips across my hand. "I had a dream last night," she says.

"About what?" I ask, leaning in to kiss the base of her throat and following her bare skin to the side of her breast. She's naked under the sheet, and I gather her against me, my hand skimming the back of her bare leg.

"About us," she says, kissing my ear and then my mouth.

We kiss for a minute or more before I say, "Were we doing this in your dream?"

She smiles and says, "I think we had done this. And a lot more, actually."

"That's my favorite kind of dream," I say, sliding her on top of me. I know every inch, every curve, every soft spot of her. But I don't think I'll ever grow tired of feeling her against me, of the knowledge that we fit as if we were made for each other.

She makes a soft sound of pleasure, and then says near my ear, "It may not be a dream."

"It's definitely not one right now," I agree, laughing.

"I think we might have made a baby, Ren."

I go completely still. "What did you say?"

"A baby. Would that be a good dream?" she asks, and I hear the slight note of uncertainty in her voice.

"That would be an incredible dream," I say softly. "The best dream ever."

"I'm late," she says. "Like really late."

"Seriously?"

"Very."

She's looking down at me now with the kind of love in her eyes that I once doubted I would ever deserve. It's the kind of love that makes me want to give her every good part of myself, to earn her love every day of my life.

"Can we buy one of those stick things today?" I ask.

She laughs. "Yes, we can buy a stick thing."

"And then we'll know?"

"We should," she says.

I lean in and kiss her, hoping I'm able to convey everything I feel for her. And I think I do, because I feel the tears sliding down her cheeks.

"Hey," I say, brushing them away.

"Happy tears," she says.

We look at each other for several long moments before she says, "Think we could name the baby Colby? Boy or girl."

Now I'm the one with tears in my eyes. "Do you have any idea how much I love you?"

"I think I do. Amazingly enough," she says. "But you could show me anyway. Before we go get the stick thing, I mean."

"Well, that would absolutely be my pleasure," I say, pulling my wife to me and showing her in the one way that doesn't need a single word to be understood.

More Books by Inglath Cooper

Swerve

The Heart That Breaks

My Italian Lover

Fences – Book Three – Smith Mountain Lake Series

Dragonfly Summer – Book Two – Smith Mountain Lake
Series

Blue Wide Sky – Book One – Smith Mountain Lake
Series

That Month in Tuscany

And Then You Loved Me

Down a Country Road

Good Guys Love Dogs

Truths and Roses

Nashville – Part Ten – Not Without You

Nashville – Book Nine – You, Me and a Palm Tree

Nashville – Book Eight – R U Serious

Nashville – Book Seven – Commit

Nashville – Book Six – Sweet Tea and Me

Nashville – Book Five – Amazed

MORE BOOKS BY INGLATH COOPER

Nashville – Book Four – Pleasure in the Rain
Nashville – Book Three – What We Feel
Nashville – Book Two – Hammer and a Song
Nashville – Book One – Ready to Reach
On Angel's Wings
A Gift of Grace
RITA® Award Winner John Riley's Girl
A Woman With Secrets
Unfinished Business
A Woman Like Annie
The Lost Daughter of Pigeon Hollow
A Year and a Day

Dear Reader:

I would like to thank you for taking the time to read my story. There are so many wonderful books to choose from these days, and I am hugely appreciative that you chose mine.

Please join my mailing list for updates on new releases and giveaways! Just go to http://www.inglathcooper.com – come check out my Facebook page for postings on books, dogs and things that make life good!

Wishing you many, many happy afternoons of reading pleasure.

All best,

Inglath

About Inglath Cooper

RITA® Award-winning author Inglath Cooper was born in Virginia. She is a graduate of Virginia Tech with a degree in English. She fell in love with books as soon as she learned how to read. "My mom read to us before bed, and I think that's how I started to love stories. It was like a little mini-vacation we looked forward to every night before going to sleep. I think I eventually read most of the books in my elementary school library."

That love for books translated into a natural love for writing and a desire to create stories that other readers could get lost in, just as she had gotten lost in her favorite books. Her stories focus on the dynamics of relationships, those between a man and a woman, mother and daughter, sisters, friends. They most often take place in small Virginia towns very much like the one where she grew up and are peopled with characters who reflect those values and traditions.

"There's something about small-town life that's just part of who I am. I've had the desire to live in other places, wondered what it would be like to be a true Manhattanite, but the thing

I know I would miss is the familiarity of faces everywhere I go. There's a lot to be said for going in the grocery store and seeing ten people you know!"

Inglath Cooper is an avid supporter of companion animal rescue and is a volunteer and donor for the Franklin County Humane Society. She and her family have fostered many dogs and cats that have gone on to be adopted by other families. "The rewards are endless. It's an eye-opening moment to realize that what one person throws away can fill another person's life with love and joy."

Follow Inglath on Facebook

at www.facebook.com/inglathcooperbooks

Join her mailing list for news of new releases and giveaways at www.inglathcooper.com

Get in Touch With Inglath Cooper

Email: inglathcooper@gmail.com
  Facebook – Inglath Cooper Books
  Instagram – inglath.cooper.books
  Pinterest – Inglath Cooper Books
  Twitter – InglathCooper

CPSIA information can be obtained
at www.ICGtesting.com
Printed in the USA
LVHW012103081219
639845LV00008B/332/P

9 780578 441498